Tempo de mercês

GRACE PERIOD

TRANSLATED FROM PORTUGUESE BY MARGARET JULL COSTA

MARIA JUDITE
DE CARVALHO

TWO LINES
PRESS

Originally published as *Tempo de mercês*
© Maria Isabel De Carvalho Tavares Rodrigues Alves Fraga, 2013
Published with special arrangements with The Ella Sher Literary Agency
Translation © 2025 by Margaret Jull Costa

Two Lines Press
www.twolinespress.com

Any use of this publication to "train" generative artificial intelligence (AI) technologies to generate text is expressly prohibited. The author reserves all rights to license uses of this work for generative AI training and development of machine learning language models.

ISBN: 978-1-949641-82-0
Ebook: 978-1-949641-83-7

Cover design by Najeebah Al-Ghadban
Cover photos: Istvan Kadar Photography/Moment via Getty Images; H. Armstrong Roberts/Retrofile RF via Getty Images
Typeset by Lola Jo

Library of Congress Cataloging-in-Publication Data
Names: Carvalho, Maria Judite de, author. | Costa, Margaret Jull, translator.
Title: Grace period / Maria Judite de Carvalho; translated from the Portuguese by Margaret Jull Costa. Other titles: Tempo de mercês. English
Description: San Francisco, CA : Two Lines Press, 2025. | "Originally published as Tempo de mercês"--Title page verso. | Identifiers: LCCN 2025000445 (print) | LCCN 2025000446 (ebook) | ISBN 9781949641820 (paperback) | ISBN 9781949641837 (epub) | Subjects: LCGFT: Novels. Classification: LCC PQ9265.A77 T4613 2025 (print) | LCC PQ9265. A77 (ebook) | DDC 869.3/42--dc23/eng/20250226 | LC record available at https://lccn.loc.gov/2025000445 | LC ebook record available at https://lccn. loc.gov/2025000446

1 3 5 7 9 10 8 6 4 2

This project is supported within the scope of the Open Call for Translation of Literary Works by the Lusa-American Development Foundation.

ALSO BY MARIA JUDITE
DE CARVALHO

EMPTY WARDROBES
SO MANY PEOPLE, MARIANA

The platform had the aggressive, melancholy air of all train stations at night, stations where no one else gets off, and more to the point, where no one is there waiting to meet us. The man stepped down from the train and stood stock still, although his thin body did sway slightly forward. He looked around for no apparent reason, because there really wasn't anything worth looking at. The dim, grubby light from the feeble lamps—incapable of penetrating the air thick with darkness and coal dust—was suddenly familiar, and this somehow made things easier. All his life he had thought of that light as peculiar to train stations. The smell too, an old, you might say, well-preserved smell, a mixture of burned coal and flowers in full bloom, flowers that constantly grow and die, and, for hours or days, are just that, flowers, in the small, neat flowerbeds of the time. Were they carnations? Or Wisteria? Would there be Wisteria in June? Spring was over, but... He thought he could hear a loud, sneering voice crowing delightedly over his general ignorance. "Wisteria (or any other flower), in June (or any other month)!" All at once, he felt extraordinarily alone and impotent, and set off with slow, reticent steps, as if he had no real goal, walking beside a time long gone, colorful, cheerful, and pretty, above all pretty, past a row of tourist posters praising the pleasant climate, the lush green countryside, the calm sea, and the simple habits of the kindly locals. Anyway, the sky was still blue and the locals were still welcoming. Even more so, given how tourism had grown in recent years. Or so they said.

The hotel was in the square opposite the station, and that's where he headed. There's always a hotel in the square opposite every station, or did he only think this because of that hotel? It was called Terminus, because the owner had once made a trip abroad, Terminus in very intense, bright lights, the letters united by a bright halo. That had been its name before. Initially, though—the man recalled people saying—it had been the Travelers' Inn.

"I'd like a room, if I may," he said at reception,

and he used those exact words because it always seemed to him that even when he was paying for things—bought or rented—the seller was making an exception for him, doing him a favor, rather than giving him what was simply his due. "One that isn't too expensive," he added. "It's only for a day or two, three at most," he explained, as if he were defending his reputation. "Possibly only until tomorrow afternoon…" he said, because he was an honest fellow.

The man at the reception desk wore a look that was half-suspicious, half-friendly (his eyes were suspicious, while his mouth smiled), and, as if he hadn't heard him, he said:

"Do you have a reservation? Your name please."

"Well, no, I don't, I didn't think it necessary…"

There was a sigh, a weary gesture.

"We have far too many guests. Even in winter. In June, we have to turn away twenty or thirty people a day."

"I didn't know that. So that means…"

"I'm afraid so."

"Fine…"

He was about to leave, but the receptionist picked up a book and leafed through it. "Actually, we do happen to have a vacant room," he said. "Purely by chance. The only one in the entire hotel. The guest, a German gentleman, had a phone call from Munich and left this very afternoon. It's one of our best rooms too. Would that suit you? It has a bathroom and a sea view."

"Yes, that would suit me," said the man, feeling suddenly overcome by weariness, like someone finding a place to sit at the end of a long walk. "That would suit me perfectly."

The smile then won the duel and overcame that earlier suspicious look, generously revealing some rather uneven yellow teeth. "Here's the key," the receptionist said in a slightly flutey, almost tender voice, an *ihr sehr ergebener*—your devoted servant— voice. As if the man were the German gentleman from Munich. Which was not the case. Which was certainly not the case.

A boy in a crumpled uniform picked up both suitcase and key, which the man had forgotten to take, and set off up the stairs, having first explained that the elevator had been out of order for nearly a week and, since there was no local tradesman who could repair it, they'd had to send for someone from Lisbon. Still, as long as they got it fixed… It was such a nuisance.

Nuisance was the right word, said the man in solidarity, going up the stairs with him. Meanwhile, he was thinking that the staircase was very different from how he remembered it as a child. It was less majestic, not as broad; the gilding in the foyer downstairs wasn't as gilded, nor were the Ficus plants as green and glossy, and the china pots they stood in were badly cracked, with soil leaking out from the cracks.

Stepping slowly, lightly, one might almost say ceremoniously, he walked up the very worn red runner. It was as if he was aware of the important fact that he was finally meeting someone whom he had admired from afar for many years, someone who was finally opening her heart to him, or at least, her arms. Alas, the heart of a hotel is cold and distant. Its arms can be bought by anyone. Some people love hotels for that very reason; there's no need to pretend with them, he thought, everything is simple and inconsequential.

"Incredibly hot, isn't it?" said the boy in a friendly manner.

"Yes," said the man in a flat voice, lacking the strength or the desire to be more expressive. "Imagine what it's like in Lisbon."

"Like an oven."

"Here there's always a sea breeze. And there's swimming of course."

"Oh, yes, that really helps."

The key—attached to a big, heavy star that reminded him of the starfish his father had found once at low tide, and that he'd kept for years in a drawer with other fossils (whatever happened to them?)—turned in the lock, and the door slowly opened. Suddenly, the room was too large for that man accustomed to more modest rooms. It was also too luxurious, and this troubled him a little and gave him a slight twinge of conscience. Despite everything. A vast double bed with a dark red bedspread, a closet, a dressing-table/desk, curtains the same color as the bedspread, a huge rug.

The boy put the suitcase down on the wooden bench, walked diagonally across the room to open a second door on the right. "The bathroom," he announced with a sweep of his hand. Then he went over to the head of the bed. "Here's the bell for the maid. The phone goes straight through to reception." He walked back and paused at the first door, which still stood open. "And before you leave the hotel tomorrow, would you mind filling out the form? Do you need anything else?"

That "anything else" was unnecessary, because he hadn't yet needed anything at all, apart from being left alone and, it's true, finding out the name of those flowers with the intense, old-fashioned perfume. This, though, had been a momentary desire, quickly abandoned in the middle of the platform. The only thing that lasted was seeing the door close on the four walls of that unfamiliar room, having a bath, and lying down to read—a little—the newspaper he'd bought in Lisbon and not opened during the journey. He saw only that the room cost 250 *escudos* and bore the number 127. And he opened the closet, which was as empty as a tomb, apart from its varnished semi-skeletons waiting to be clothed. Then he abandoned himself to the arms of the hotel.

In the morning, he shaved and ordered breakfast—"Continental?" He had no idea. Coffee and bread and butter—then he got dressed, taking great pains over his appearance. He knew from experience how important it was to be well-groomed, which is why he always brought with him a small rectangle of thick wool and a stiff brush to polish his shoes. Every night, when he got undressed, he would smooth the crease in his pants and drape them slowly, precisely, over the hanger.

He studied himself in the mirror, touching his face, a habit that always made Alberta smile. As if he were seeking the invisible in the visible. "It's there, man, it won't run away from you!" her loud voice had said one day, the voice that, at least in part, dominated his existence. And afterward, whenever he raised his hand to his face, he always thought that, yes, it really was there.

He went down the stairs and across the foyer, where the receptionist smiled at him, now entirely unsuspiciously, from behind the counter, which hadn't been there before, and which was adorned with miniature copper utensils and dolls in traditional dress.

The man said, "Good morning," and handed him the key. The receptionist asked in a friendly manner if he had slept well.

"Very well, thank you."

"Rather hot, though."

"Oh, I don't mind the heat."

"It's going to be a lovely day."

"The weather's usually good in June."

"Not always," said the receptionist. "Not always. A few years ago, we had such torrential rain that some guests even left."

"Only to be expected."

"No, it's most unusual."

"I mean that it's only to be expected that some guests would leave."

"Ah, yes, you're right. Here's the form."

The man filled it out slowly and methodically.

He left the hotel, skirted around it, and found himself on the long, meandering street that changes its name whenever it narrows, calls itself a square when it opens out again, and divides the town into two unequal parts; the narrowest part leads down to the old fishing port, now a harbor for hovercraft and motorboats (although the man didn't know this); while the other part climbs up the nearby hills, scattering a few white houses here and there, first on the scrub it passes through and, later, among the cultivated fields. He hesitated, unsure as to which direction to take. He felt he should turn right, but was that really where he needed to go? He thought hard. If he continued along until he came to the first side street, then turned left, heading away from the sea, he might manage to orient himself. The town wasn't that big, and he wasn't that old. What he needed was a reference point.

He decided to go left, and set off slowly, as if he, too, had no appointments to keep or problems to resolve, as if he were allowing himself, as once he had, to drift on the serene waters of the tame, domesticated, odorless sea. It was only ten o'clock, but it must already have been hot, as he realized from the fact that nearly everyone else was walking around scantily clad. Women in shorts, men in open-neck shirts.

At one point, a bottle top appeared next to the toe of his shoe. This ruffled the calm surface of the waters, and out of them emerged an initially extremely fluid image, which gradually grew more defined until it became that of a small boy, his hands in the pockets of shorts that were always a size too big (by the time they did begin to fit him, they would be worn out), kicking the bottle top down the street and silently shouting with all his might: *g-o-o-a-l*! The boy was walking down the street, down this street, bare-chested because it was so hot, perhaps in July or August. He was whistling some song or other that was popular at the time. An English song or an American one. Ginho had the record. Ginho had a few records and a fantastic record player, one of those wind-up ones. You wound it up and the record would start to play. And when, at the end, it began to wind down again, that always made everyone crack up laughing.

The man stopped for a moment to think about the song that time had melted away, though not completely (a song about ferryboats, lovers, the moon, and concertinas), and then about the heat. It seemed to him that heat used to be more important, or, rather, more pressing. But perhaps this was because he had grown used to being hot, or for other reasons, and it was no longer so important to him. In those days, the heat had been a really big thing, almost all-consuming. His mother would complain in her plangent voice, smiling the bitter smile that, for some reason, he always found so troubling, and that seemed to be accusing him of something, possibly of merely existing. "If I could at least go down to the esplanade and sit there for a while and rest…" That had been her great ambition—or so he had believed for a long time—her idea of near-happiness, sitting on an esplanade, leisurely sipping a cool drink through a straw, observing who else was there and who came and went. Right up until the end. Because, when, in her later years, she could afford to work less, she no longer knew how to relax. She was like a machine plugged into a socket. Not a happy machine, like Alberta used to be, but hesitant and creaky.

That half-naked boy would drink the iced water the waiter at the Café Flor do Mar would give him for free in a big, heavy glass, its sides all wet and bearing the white image of a daisy or a sailboat, and then he would go through the archway in the wall down to the beach to dive into a wave, if there were any waves, but none of this brought him any lasting comfort. It was as if everything were burning—but without flames or wind—the air, the houses, the people, even their thoughts, melted to nothing in the heat. "It's so hot, I've never known a summer like it," the others would say earnestly, the people he knew then, the grown-ups. He would say nothing, but then he never did say much. He would set off down the street, tooting his horn, tires screeching around the bends, speeding down the esplanade at eighty miles an hour in his fabulous invisible Renault, then he would park, get out, and race down the sandy slope to plunge headfirst into that amazingly calm, almost drowsy, almost warm sea. On some days, there wasn't even a ribbon of foam edging the waves, which would break on the sand, blending in to form a brief colorless zone. At other times, he would swim out to where he could no longer touch the bottom and let himself float, eyes open, nose in the air; indeed, sometimes at night, once they had turned out the light and told him "Go to sleep now," he felt as if he were lying in some soft maternal substance, neither air nor water, certainly not a mattress, and would fall asleep like that, arms flung wide. He didn't always drive the Renault that no one, apart from Ginho, could see. "What kind of idiot are you?" the other boys would ask. He would also walk, very slowly, hands in his pockets, hair in his eyes. Do the fish feel the heat, he would think. Then: No, of course they don't. They're cold-blooded. "You need to be cold-blooded at all times," his father would say. What, like the fish, the boy he was at the time would wonder. Then he would think: If I had a motorboat… The count had one… Why do some people have one and others not? He considered this thought to be very profound and original. Now, at thirty-five, he still considered it to be original, although without realizing it.

A bottle top, and his thoughts immediately stopped. Action took over—*g-o-o-a-l*—and the top would be catapulted forward, to hit a wall or the legs of some passerby. Sometimes it wasn't a bottle top, but a cork with a hole in it, an old matchbox, or nothing at all. Empty space. The small boy would kick out at nothing. The biggest kicks, the ones that hit the target, were the ones he found most consoling.

He went to a newsstand, where he paused to look at the goods for sale. From the rotating display stand he chose a postcard, intending to send it to Alberta after lunch. It might arrive before he did, or it might not. Either way, she would be pleased. He chose the one with the bluest sea and the most golden rocks, and in the foreground, a very tanned woman wearing a white bikini; then he asked how much it was and paid, before asking rather hesitantly:

"Could you tell me where Rua da Palmeira is?"

The clerk came out from behind the counter of the newsstand.

"Keep going as far as the first street on your left, Rua de São Paulo Estreita, then continue on down. When you reach a square with a pillar in the middle, take the street immediately ahead of you, to the right. There's another one to the left, but that's not it. The town hall stands in between the two. It's the one on the right."

"I see…"

"You can't go wrong. Take a left, go as far as the square, and Rua da Palmeira is straight ahead. It's a short street, you can't go wrong."

The man was about to say, "Yes, a short street, I know it well," but remained silent, as if embarrassed by what he hadn't said, purely for having thought it, because it would be inappropriate or, at the very least, odd, after he had just asked her for directions. Instead, because it suddenly seemed important, he asked if there was, in fact, a palm tree on that street.

"I don't know," she said. For the first time, her face showed some expression, and she smiled like someone suddenly struck by a very silly thought. "Do you know, I've never noticed. I was born here, and yet it's never occurred to me to see if there's a palm tree on Rua da Palmeira. I mean, there should be one, shouldn't there, with a name like that…"

The man thanked her. "My pleasure," she said, adding, "It's going to be a hot day."

"Yes," said the man automatically.

He went down the side street as she had told

him to, and immediately began to recognize things. A cheap eatery—an eatery, that's what they called it then—now it was a snack bar full of glass (mirrors, areas divided into two- and four-tops) and white metal furniture; the Amado drugstore, where he used to go for his calcium injections, and which had also been updated; the small scrap-metal shop had gone upmarket too and was now Chez something-or-other, a store selling knickknacks and local souvenirs. The Count's summer residence, whitewashed like nearly all the houses in the town, was taller than most, with a very ornate chimney stack that dominated the other chimneys (the nearby ones, of course), and rather ostentatious green balconies protecting the large French windows. What was the Count's full name? the man thought. Would the little boy ever have known? Almost certainly not. He was simply the Count. "Today I saw the Count and the Count's wife," he said over supper, having first devoured his soup. "You mean the *Countess*," said his father, correcting him. "It's about time you started to speak properly, you're certainly old enough." His mother broke in to ask, intrigued, in one of those sudden, fleeting flashes of curiosity that sometimes gripped her: "What was she wearing? I haven't seen her for ages." Then she added accusingly, "But then, of course, I never leave the house. Only in the morning, to go shopping, and at that hour, she's still in bed." There was a bitter little crease at each corner of her downturned mouth, a crease he had recently begun to notice around Alberta's mouth too. "Come on, tell me!" and her words sounded harsh. Besides, it was a difficult question. The boy never noticed—well, would any boy his age?—what people were wearing. This was something only grown-ups cared about. But his mother was waiting, and her dark eyes seemed to grow still darker and larger, as they did whenever his father was late to come home, and she looked at him like that, with those urgent, anxious eyes, waiting for an explanation that never came, because one day he simply stopped coming home at all. The small boy he had once been would always lower his eyes, unable to bear her gaze even when it wasn't actually trained on him. And he never understood, not even later on when he was an adult, what the key emotion was behind that look: urgency, curiosity, anxiety, pain? He hesitated, but his mother's eyes insisted, bright and alert even now that they were dead. "She was wearing red," he said at last. "Red?" his mother said, shocked, for she herself always dressed very discreetly. "Red? Are you sure?" No, of course he wasn't sure, but because he had no other answer, he said, "Yeah, sure thing. A dress with a full skirt, really pretty, a very full skirt, Mama, and red shoes too, high heels, very high heels…" "'Sure thing?' Oh really," his father said. "When will the boy learn to speak properly?" His mother would interrupt, indeed, she did interrupt him on the particular day the man was thinking about—although quite why he didn't know—as he walked along Rua de São Paulo Estreita. "It's only natural he should forget even the little he knows. What could be more natural, given the company he keeps: Ginho, who only speaks slang, Ginho's father, who says 'dontcha,' and his mother…" His father yelled, "That's enough!" and her eyes flashed, then grew suddenly dull, dim. "Of course," she said. "Of course." She stood up—she had been sitting—and went into the house. She always did on such occasions.

The man had almost reached Largo do Pelourinho, and he could remember everything now. The stone pillar, the *pelourinho* that the square had been named after, was a modest affair, with a little parched grass around the base and some rusty railings. He didn't remember it being so short or so slender. It had seemed almost tall, tall and majestic. A really, really big pillar. He looked at the clock on the town hall and checked to see if his watch was right. It was. He had plenty of time, almost half an hour, long enough to arrange various people and objects inside himself.

A bent old lady, wrapped in a black shawl (he seemed to recognize her dark, rather Moorish face, but this momentary thought immediately vanished), walked past him, and looked at him briefly, intensely, before disappearing through a small door. The door closed quickly, noiselessly, and the cotton curtain covering the window twitched slightly, very slightly…

He smiled and continued on his way.

When he opened the front door, he felt quite moved. The first thing he noticed was the smell, the breath of the house. But what did it smell of? Dust, airlessness, the absence of any smell at all? Before, whenever the door opened, he knew at once what the smell was. Sometimes, it was his father's pipe; at others, his mother's cologne; at still others, the good lunch she was preparing. It all depended on the time of day, the hour. The hours, though, had long since ceased to be of any significance in that closed-up house. The hours, the days, and the years. It was like entering a family tomb—he was full of gloomy thoughts—a tomb with no flowers and no tears, having been abandoned twenty-five years ago, because the family had all died at the same time, and he, the one remaining member, was not the best person to watch over the dead. In fact, he had never felt very far from them, had never felt himself to be very alive or that they were very dead. The frontier between them was not clearly defined, everything was fused together, con-fused.

He closed the door, and inside there was only dust. The bones must be in a box, in a corner somewhere. The bones of his father, who died in Africa, although he had never found out how, the circumstances, the place, whether he was alone or with people; the bones of his mother, who couldn't or wouldn't or didn't want to forgive; and the bones of the small boy he had once been. Those bones.

He tried to open the living room door, but the handle came off in his hand. It was an ugly handle, old too, a stupid thing. However, he put it back where it had always been, because it was best not to leave the house in an even worse state than it already was, and so he slowly turned the handle to the left and pushed very gently. Once inside, he went over to the window, grappled with the stiff bolts on the shutters, and felt his hands grow grimy. However, he hesitated before wiping them on his handkerchief, hesitated for a long time, because he was a respecter of both handkerchiefs and memories, even when they were nothing but dust.

The ray of sunlight that rushed in—after a twenty-five-year wait outside—fell on an old rocking chair forgotten or abandoned to its fate, which the man instantly recognized: it had been his father's chair, where he would sometimes sit after supper, although only rarely, smoking his aromatic pipe. There were other things, although few in number and mostly of little value: an old rolled up rug, a broom that was more handle than broom; on the wall, in a pyro-engraved frame, an old portrait of his father's father, leaning on a column, with clouds and a kind of romantic castle in the background. He used to think it was a lovely portrait. Now, it seemed to him a suitable portrait for a tomb. That grandfather whom he had never known had been shut up there since the day he (still a small boy) had left that house for the last time with his mother. He had left, stiff and obedient, without a sad or rebellious word, but with his eyes as full of water as lakes in winter overflowing after a heavy downpour. His tears, though, had not overflowed. He knew that something very serious had happened, and that it had perhaps been his fault. Yes, it must have been his fault. Shortly before, his father had said to him, "Let this be a lesson to you, Mateus." He called him Mateus for the first and last time, and he understood that something had happened to his childhood.

That had been in the summer too, in August. He had grown taller then, and he no longer ran down the streets bare-chested because he thought it indecent or perhaps inappropriate at his age. He could also cope better with the heat, with a possibly rather affected dignity, imitating the grown-ups. He was beginning to be interested in other new, exciting things, like beating the other boys at front crawl and learning to smoke in secret with Ginho, and blowing the smoke out through his nose. From one day to the next, he had also found himself looking in a different way at the older girls, and at one particularly fascinating woman, and discovering that looking at some of them and at that one woman was both pleasant and promising.

Someone rapped on the door, quietly, reticently. Rapped, then waited. Then knocked again and again waited. Like someone knocking at the gate of eternity, and therefore in no hurry for an answer.

The man looked at his watch, surprised. But it was, in fact, time. Eleven o'clock on the dot, or rather, one minute past. He stood up—he had finally opted to sit in his father's chair, having first carefully wiped it clean of dust with his handkerchief—and went to open the front door, which was stiff because time had stiffened it.

"May I come in, Senhor Silva?" asked the person at the door.

"Yes, please do."

He was Senhor Silva. He smiled apologetically. He had never really become used to being Senhor

Silva, *the* Senhor Silva, and had always felt uncomfortable, ill at ease. "Silva, has that letter to so-and-so been sent?" his boss would ask, the boss with the loud, all-knowing voice. And, at such moments, he would always look around, as if not quite realizing that the Silva in question was him. He had never simply accepted, as others seemed to do—right away, uncritically, unthinkingly—certain facts that were, apparently, perfectly natural and normal. The name "Silva," for example, which belonged to them both, first to his father and then to him; that job where he would spend the rest of his working life (and that he had started, on a purely temporary basis, fifteen years earlier), or his own face, to which he had never completely adapted—he still felt a slight, secret, unconfessed hope that he would wake one morning with a different face, neither better nor worse, just different.

"Do come in," he said again.

The man came in.

The difference between a man who is "still young" and a man who is frankly old, is, he thought, quite astonishing. Everything has changed, apart perhaps from the eyes—which provide the pale filling for two equally pale eyelids, puffy and wrinkled—and yet, we recognize him right away, even if we weren't expecting to see him, and we give a little internal yelp both of confirmation and slight suspicion. The skin has grown looser, more shriveled, the hair thin and white, the body has shrunk in height, and, at the same time, increased, almost shockingly, in volume. And yet it is the same man.

"Do sit down, Senhor Osório," he said, leading him into what had been the living room. "Have a chair. It's a little dirty, of course, although I have already… It's just years and years of dust, but I'm afraid I have nothing better to offer you."

"Thank you, I am a little tired," said the other man in his soft, gentle voice. "I had to meet someone at the café downtown, and rushed here afterward because I always like to be punctual. As it is, I'm already two minutes late."

"Yes, two minutes."

"I can't walk very fast anymore. This wretched rheumatism won't let me. And my heart isn't as strong as it was either."

"You suffered from rheumatism before, didn't you?

The other man looked at him in amazement. "Yes, I did. Fancy you remembering."

He began to sit down, but only began, because every gesture he made—the man-who-had-been-a-child remembered this too—was slow and cautious. He treated himself as if he were a very fragile body. FRAGILE in large, capital letters. Once he was seated, the chair creaked and groaned as if it were about to break, because the new arrival was a large man, bordering on obese.

The man, the owner of the house, asked to be excused and went in search of a chair from another room. He found an old kitchen stool, slightly lame, but that served its purpose. He sat down, having first blown away the dust and wiped the seat with his handkerchief.

"How old are you, Senhor Osório?" he asked at last.

"I turned seventy-one last month. Time flies, my friend. Before we know it, we'll have one foot in the grave, isn't that right?"

That is always a question that clearly requires no answer, and is merely decorative, a rhetorical ornament. The man did not respond. Osório let the subject drop and said:

"I certainly wouldn't have recognized you, Senhor Silva."

Of course not, how could he? "Of course not," he said. "But why don't you call me Mateus? That's what you used to call me."

"I used to call you Matinho," said Osório, smiling.

"Perhaps so, yes, I think you did. Matinho."

"You were a boy then. I thought you might not like being called that now."

"Why ever not?"

There was a silence, during which both men considered speaking, then decided not to. What about your wife? Mateus was thinking. Osório must be thinking: And your parents? *Your father?*

"My father died a few years ago, in Africa," he said in response to the question he himself had thought to ask. "In Johannesburg."

"Yes, I knew that. That he had died, I mean. But no one could tell me where. For some reason, I assumed it was Brazil."

"No, he died in Johannesburg."

"Well, I never."

Another silence, then Mateus added, "And my mother died shortly afterward."

"Oh, I am sorry. I didn't know about your mother." He hesitated, then gave a short laugh.

"There I am saying *tua mãe*, calling you *tu*, just like in the old days. And what did she die of?"

What did it matter to him? Obviously so little that he was already scanning the room. What did she die of, the mother of that man, Mateus to some (very few), Silva or Senhor Silva or good old Silva to everyone else, Matinho to his mother, right up until she died? Time, however, needed to be filled, all of it, both the large, desolate expanses and the small empty spaces, and Osório knew this. That's why he asked "What did your mother die of?" in a relatively interested tone of voice, although his eyes were looking elsewhere.

"Her heart. That was her weak point. And she'd always had a difficult life, full of problems... As you know."

He said this bit by bit, slowly, his eyes fixed on Osório. Osório's gaze had returned, and he was listening with polite attention, like someone feeling very deeply, but thinking of something else.

"Well, we all have difficult lives full of problems," he said. "It depends how we deal with them. There's no escaping them though. I suppose those in the higher spheres don't approve of our lives going along too smoothly, and when our lives do, they make up for it—perhaps because, until then, they'd forgotten all about us—by dropping some huge problem on us, the apparently insoluble sort. When I say 'higher spheres,' you know what I'm getting at, don't you?"

No, Mateus didn't immediately understand, but then he had never been quick on the uptake, and he assumed initially that Osório probably meant politicians, but he nodded anyway, like someone who knows what's what, and is perfectly at home with the subject, well, relatively so. Meanwhile, he was thinking that Osório didn't speak badly at all, as his mother always used to say he did, he even spoke a rather refined Portuguese. Would he still say "dontcha"? He really needed to know.

"And…your family?" he asked with some effort.

"Oh, not too bad," Osório said casually. "My wife has very high blood pressure, and with me it's the rheumatism. See how bent my fingers are? The damp sea air doesn't help, but this is where my life is, so what can I do? Jorge became a doctor, you know. He still sometimes talks about you. He would have loved to meet up with you, but he's abroad at the moment, at a conference. We got a postcard from him yesterday, from Rome, a postcard of the

Vatican. Then he's off to Germany."

"Excellent," said Mateus. "I'm sorry not to see him too."

Was he? asked his unconscious mind indignantly. Was he sorry? Why would Jorge be glad to see him or he Jorge? The small boy he had been and the boy the same age who was then called Ginho used to go swimming together, used to race along in their invisible cars (Ginho's was a yellow Citroen), and, in their last year together, would ogle the girls who came to spend the vacation there. He was a good lad, Ginho. Then, that summer, he, Mateus, had left never to return. His mother had pulled up stakes (his father had already headed off into the unknown—to Johannesburg, he found out later on), and the house had been left empty. Then the dust descended, and silence took hold of all those square feet of empty space.

One night, years ago, he had spotted Ginho at the movies. A tall, handsome man who bore a striking resemblance to *her*, sitting beside a pretty, dark woman wearing far too much makeup. Mateus was also with someone. She, though, was of no importance, he just happened to be there with her; perhaps the same applied to Jorge's companion. But both women were present and real, which is why the friends had simply waved enthusiastically to each other from a distance. Besides, when he thought about it, had Jorge really recognized him? He, of course, had recognized him, but then his life had very few principal characters... It may be that Jorge hadn't been able to locate him in time and space, and his wide smile and friendly wave hadn't really been directed at him, Mateus Silva, or Matinho as he used to be, but at a face smiling at him in the crowd, a familiar face with no name attached, a friend from school or college, or a patient perhaps.

"He came up with the idea," said Osório.

"What idea?"

"Buying the house. He heard that you wanted to sell. He met someone, the notary I suppose. And yet here I am, living right next door, and I knew nothing about it." He paused and looked around him sadly, then said, "It's really gone downhill, hasn't it? Dontcha agree?

"It certainly has," said Mateus, feeling suddenly much calmer.

"When was the last time you were here?"

"I left twenty-five years ago."

"And never came back."

"Never."

Osório's face grew serious. "Goodness!" he exclaimed. "Twenty-five years is a long time. Goodness me!"

"It is, isn't it?"

Osório took a crumpled pack of cigarettes out of his pocket, very carefully selected one—as if the others might be tainted or even rotten—then said, "Oh, sorry, do you smoke?"

"No, I stopped ages ago."

"And you succeeded. I've tried, but I always go back to them. What can I do? I don't drink, I avoid fatty foods, so a little cigarette now and then…"

There was a pause, which Mateus filled by feeling his own face, or, rather, his skull. Osório took up the conversation again.

"Still in Lisbon then?"

"Yes, still there."

"When Jorge graduated, we thought of going to live there too. Sometimes you need a change of scene, dontcha think? I could sell the properties we have here and the house—because, thanks to tourism, any property near the sea has shot up in value—and buy a few properties there. The factory takes care of itself now. In the end, though, I stayed. Jorge always comes back to spend the vacations here; he's still got his motorboat, and, as he says, it's a really lively place in summer."

"It always used to be, and I imagine it still is, well, probably even more so. The Hotel Terminus…"

"A real dump!" said Osório dismissively. "The Miramar and the Marítimo, now they're really good hotels, new, and with all the modern conveniences."

Osório's eyes were indefatigably scanning the walls of what had been the living room. "Everything looks so old," he commented. "I never thought it would look so old."

"It is what it is," said Mateus, feeling suddenly tired and reluctant to play the salesman.

"If it's all like this…"

"I don't know, I haven't seen the rest of the house, but there's no reason why it won't be."

Osório gave him a puzzled look. "You haven't seen it?" he asked.

"Not for twenty-five years, and what I saw then…"

"But what about now?"

"Oh, I only just got here. Barely enough time to get a quick first impression."

"I see." Osório's eyes wrinkled, or, rather, the

skin around them did, his forehead filled with a thousand lines, and his soft lower lip swallowed his upper lip as he pondered this idea.

"What was I saying?"

Mateus shrugged. "I'm not sure. I think you were talking about the house, saying how old it looked, yes, that was it."

"Exactly. How very old it looks, and how I'd never imagined it would be in such a state. How much are you asking for it by the way? Jorge mentioned eighty *contos*. You'd be lucky. I haven't even seen the rest, but it seems to me you'd be better off demolishing it. It's the land that's valuable. And, as you know, it's not in the best location. Maybe if it was in a different part of town. Dontcha agree? Would you mind showing me the other rooms?"

Of course he wouldn't, that was why he was there. He stood up, went over to the door and turned to the right, down the dark, narrow corridor. "This way," he said.

The first room had been his parents'. Empty of furniture, it looked enormous to him, and sad too. Osório glanced around, screwing up his eyes because so little light came in through the fanlight over the door to the living room.

Osório said scornfully. "Hm, an interior room. I didn't think they existed anymore. I was told…"

"Who by?"

"I can't remember now. Anyway, someone who knew you and used to come here. Some friend of your father's perhaps. So, the house…"

"Come and see the other rooms."

The room next door was larger, and the window he flung wide opened onto a small courtyard, where, in the late afternoon, the light from a near-horizontal sun—as if wearily about to take its rest—used to flood in. He had come a long way in order to sell all these things: the late sun in the room where he had slept as a boy; his childhood memories; and the image of his father, which only had any kind of reality and consistency there in that house, a house from which he had mostly been absent. All that remained in that empty room was the wallpaper, all tiny, faded blue flowers, stained black with damp near the ceiling, and peeling off in places to hang like the fronds of a palm tree struck by lightning. The man half-closed his eyes and tried to picture the old furniture, but that image soon vanished, and his gaze found only a spider's web (had the spider died too?) where the wall met the ceiling, from the center of which hung an electric cable and a forgotten light fixture condemned to eternal darkness.

"It's a good room," he said. "Well, it was once. Spacious. Plenty of sun." His words were not words of praise. Mere description.

"Yes," said Osório. "Yes…" but he hesitated as to what to say next. "You could probably do something with the place, but, God, it would cost a lot!"

"Next door is the bathroom. A bit primitive of course. The bath's rather small, well, I suppose it seems small now; in those days, though, it seemed a decent enough size."

"In those days…ah, in those days!" Osório swept the air with one plump, very hairy little hand, its ring finger adorned with a large diamond ring. "It's the size of the house that matters," he said. "And the light. As well as the state it's in, of course. The rest is just stuff." And he swept that stuff aside with a wide, definitive gesture, as the man, Mateus Silva, silently opened the door at the end of the corridor to reveal a dark, gloomy kitchen with a blackened iron stove standing on a yellowing stone base.

A glossy, black cockroach ran toward them, startled. "What on earth can a cockroach find to eat in a deserted house?" Mateus said out loud.

"No idea," cried Osório, roughly pushing open the window, then trying to lean out a little farther, which was far from easy because the window was really open little more than a crack. "Graça! Graça!" he called. And his voice wavered, unable to keep up the necessary volume. "Gra-a-a-ç-a!"

"Do you want to go out in the garden?"

"No, it's not worth it. Gra-a-a-ç-a!"

Somewhere out there, beyond the wall, another window opened, and the man heard a very familiar voice: "Is that you? Where are you?"

Mateus concentrated hard on that voice, Graça's voice, which was the same even after twenty-five years, with no wrinkles, no worry lines, resistant to time and to storms. Storms? he thought. Storms… There had certainly been storms in the house, with shipwrecks and lost lives and property, but in that other house…

Osório somehow managed to stick his head still farther out. His body was all contorted, would it be possible to actually climb out of that window? "I'm here, up here!" he said in a voice that kept trying to rise in volume, only to succumb, incapable of making the effort. "I'm here next door. Just to tell you that our friend will be having supper with us."

Somewhat embarrassed, Mateus wondered if by "our friend" Osório meant him? Should he say "No" right away, thanking him for the invitation, but explaining that he would prefer to have supper at the hotel? But what if "our friend" was someone else? Then it might look as if he were inviting himself. No, there could be no doubt that it was him. This was so typical of Osório, he remembered now, recognizing his style: "Our friend Abílio will be having supper with us, Graça," before he had said so much as a word to Abílio, Mateus's father.

"I hope you don't have some prior engagement," Osório said, extricating himself from the window.

"Well, I was thinking I'd just take a little stroll around town, have a late supper, and go right to bed. Besides, I don't have anything nice to wear and…"

"Oh, don't worry about what to wear, man. It's just a matter of setting another place at the table. I told Graça because she doesn't like having to make last-minute arrangements, but you won't mind something simple, will you?"

The window next door closed, but Osório took a while to resume their conversation, continuing to study the garden intently. Mateus could also remember a time when the garden had been a proper garden, full of scented flowerbeds, but that—little by little, as slowly as the anxiety that would gradually fill his mother's eyes—was overtaken by invasive weeds or other unwanted things. Unwanted? What about the lizards? It became a paradise for lizards, of course. And as a little boy, how he had loved to sit, looking for them, keeping very still and quiet. A small, stiff head with bright little eyes would suddenly emerge, followed by a tense, gray-green body, like a dry, pointed leaf, but so alert and alive, so ready for action, even when it appeared to be sleeping, and filled with such an amazing zest for life, such an incredible will to live, even when life was slipping away. One day, he'd managed to catch one in a trap he'd made. That had been an amazing day, Ginho and the others had come to see it, and, unbeknownst to his mother, he even took the lizard up to his bedroom and kept it there for a few days, feeding it insects he caught specially. He wanted to make it a pet, but hadn't succeeded. He couldn't remember now if the lizard escaped or died, if he was the one to set it free or if he even gave the matter any thought.

"Will you look at the state of the place!" Osório said, and he sounded as if it really pained him to say this. "Dreadful! People are so strange. I can't understand how you…" He hesitated, then plunged headfirst into concrete facts. "I don't imagine you're exactly rolling in money, otherwise you wouldn't be selling the house."

"I'm selling it because I need to."

"That's exactly what I was saying, or, rather, thinking of saying. Since you're clearly not loaded, why didn't you sell the house years ago, or rent it out? You could have had some work done, and then found a tenant. Twenty-five years is a long time."

He shrugged, and nothing more was said. There was no point explaining to this man, Osório, that his father had only died ten years ago and that, for those last ten years, it had been enough just knowing that he had that land, that roof, and it might have been enough for the rest of his life, if, of course, he didn't have a good reason to sell, which was, in a way, now the case. Not mentioning it, not even thinking about it, simply knowing the house existed and was his. This detail saved everything else from being a total disaster, and at least gave him some confidence in the future. A little patch of land that was all his in this big, wide world. A few dozen square feet that belonged to him, to Mateus Silva. He would sometimes think—although only rarely—that people didn't understand how important that was. They rented their piece of ground, or their floor, month by month, and one day, suddenly, they had nowhere to live. "I have my house should I ever need it. And I can walk around, I can go to bed, I can do whatever I like, there in my house, on my piece of land. It's locked up and empty, waiting for me." That's what he would think, albeit fairly infrequently, and the existence of the house was more of a reassuring sensation than a motive for daydreams, however consoling.

"A long time!" Osório said again. "Yes, sir, twenty-five years isn't the same as twenty-five days."

No, it wasn't. Mateus went ahead of him into the deserted, inhospitable dining room.

"The place is falling to pieces!" Osório exclaimed, clearly troubled, and his voice echoed around the room, perhaps climbing the walls stained with the damp of many winters, stains that regrouped on the ceiling, and descended via the electrical wire that someone had cut. The crumbling plaster from the ceiling-rose formed a large, whitish circle on the floor. "It's in a dreadful state! To make it habitable again, you'd have to, well..." He opened his arms wide in a hopeless gesture. "God knows how much that would cost! The trouble is that now… It really might be best just to demolish it and build a new house. Look at the walls and the ceiling. It's raining inside, can you see? Can't you smell the damp? I wouldn't be surprised to find that the woodwork was all rotten too."

"I have no idea," muttered Mateus, but his mind was elsewhere, having stopped on a word he'd heard earlier but not noticed, which only now rang alarm bells. "Demolish," Osório had said. And he felt suddenly confused. To demolish the house would be like killing his father all over again, the only father he'd known, the one who had lived there briefly, in passing, in between his job at the Council, the café Flor do Mar, and the house next door owned by José Osório and his wife. It would also mean killing the small boy he had been at the time, and, in a way, his mother, too, as she was then, when she still liked to dab herself with perfume and sit on the esplanade to admire the Countess's clothes, the mother who, then—or always?—had looked at his father with those large, dark eyes, growing larger and darker by the day, as if they were burning her up, consuming her gaunt face. On the other hand, he needed the money urgently, it was a matter of life and death. Life *and* death? He hesitated. No, definitely death. Because a few *contos de réis* could, if nothing else, help someone to die feeling slightly happier, slightly consoled.

"So, you're really considering demolishing the house?" he asked, feigning indifference.

"What else can I do? The house is slowly crumbling, dontcha agree, my friend? I had thought of leaving my house to Jorge and this one to Natália. As I think I mentioned, they both love spending the summers here. They find the town very lively then. But I really don't know. The other little houses I own aren't so well located, they're farther away from the sea. And some of my tenants are very stubborn, the kind who'll only leave feet first."

Who was Natália? Perhaps a late addition to the family, thought Mateus while he suggested they take a look at the pantry, at an old junk room, or the attic that was accessed via a ladder that could be hooked up to the rectangular opening in the hall ceiling.

Osório glanced upward, tempted, but then reluctantly said, no, it wasn't worth it, he'd seen enough. And he took the opportunity to comment that the ceiling was too high. "That's not how rooms are built anymore. In the old days, my friend, people liked height. The rooms could be tiny, but they wanted lots of space above their heads. Now everything is functional, isn't that what they call it?" That "they" placed him and Mateus outside. Poor people don't belong to any particular age, he thought. "They" were Jorge and Natália, since there was now a Natália.

"Well, my friend, I'll be off. Tomorrow we'll sort out the paperwork. Eighty you say? I reckon that's a bit high, but…"

"Eighty."

"Fine. I mean…it's not really worth that much, but we've agreed. Eighty it is. And don't forget to come over this evening. A quarter to eight."

"I'll be there."

"Graça will be so pleased to see you. I won't invite you over just now because she won't have had time to get dressed up, and you know what women are like."

They were both standing outside the front door and José Osório seemed to be suddenly lost in thought. "Do you still remember her?" he asked. Then, without waiting for an answer, he added:

"You'll find she's changed a lot. She's put on weight."

"Well, we all change, and twenty-five years is a lifetime."

"For many people it's more than that."

"Indeed."

He lunched alone among groups of chatty, fair-haired, sun-drenched people. At the next table, two French women were inviting a waiter who resembled Alain Delon—and knew it—to go on a boat trip with them. Mateus slowly sipped his coffee, unable to ignore that conversation, which was growing saucier by the minute, then he went up to his room to escape the hottest hours of the day or perhaps simply because he didn't know what else to do. He reread yesterday's newspaper, lay down for a while, recalling other rooms in much cheaper hotels, in second- or third-rate boarding houses, in modest (although, in some cases, once-wealthy) private houses. Middle-aged ladies, widowed, divorced, or spinsters with little money because their fathers had squandered their fortune, would rent out their best room—the one with a window onto the street or one with its own entrance—to help pay the rent or to pay it all. "Senhor Silva is just like one of the family," they would say. "So polite, so undemanding, a delight. He never complains. How easy life would be if everyone was like him." Sometimes, for whatever reason, he would have to leave, and he would again have to resort to placing a small ad in the *Diário de Notícias*. "Polite gentleman…" or "Respectable gentleman…" One day, the lady who took him in as a lodger was neither old nor ugly. Nor was she very young or very beautiful. She may have been—and almost certainly was—older than him. Thirty-eight? Forty? He didn't know. She was, though, on the cusp of that poignantly uncertain age resembling a farewell. Her pale eyes and hair were of no definite shade, as if something had removed from them all light or color. Her smile was only ever a suggestion, never becoming a proper smile, and she had a quavery voice. She could easily have gone unnoticed—she could, quite rightly, be described as dull—and she had the strange ability to be present without anyone noticing. "You would have made an excellent spy," he said to her once, and only later realized that he might have hurt her feelings. She had laughed though and said, "I sometimes wonder if I would even leave any fingerprints. That's possible, don't you think?"

Her name was Albertina, but everyone had called her Alberta ever since she was a girl. She had no family at all. No children (she was infertile), no husband (he had left her), no relatives, all of whom had died when their time came, or perhaps a little earlier than expected. All she had was a nephew of her husband's, a vague kind of in-law. Perhaps that's why (although who can know why people love or don't love someone?) she had fallen in love with him. Two beings, alone in the world, thrown together? The fact that no other man had appeared in her life since her husband left? Or some other reason. It was best not to probe too deeply into the reasons why and simply to accept them with a light heart. The man had accepted them, largely because he had begun to love her too, in his fashion of course, without great enthusiasm, but sincerely. A considered, logical love, with, it's true, a touch of inevitability about it. They didn't get married because she was still married to that other man, who had one day hurriedly packed his bags and left. Like his father, thought Mateus, because although his mother had been the one to "abandon the marital home," he always saw his father as the one who had left. He had always been leaving, every day, always.

Alberta was too frank. Just as she never wore makeup, she was equally incapable of embellishing the facts, her facts. "My husband left because he suddenly grew bored with me. Perhaps he was emotionally unstable, I don't know, I didn't have time to find out. Or perhaps he was bored for the whole two years we lived together," she told him right at the start, once the time for confessions had arrived. Hadn't she tried to stop him? he asked. She looked him in the eye then: "Stop him, you mean arrest him, like a policewoman?" Then she lowered her eyes. "I know what you mean, of course, I'm not that stupid, but I just couldn't. I rather admire anyone who could. Besides, I wanted to go back to living alone. I'd always enjoyed that. Not that I'm so content with my own company; no, it's more a matter of convenience really. I'm a working woman who likes her comforts." She had fallen silent then, gazing vaguely around her, and making that very typical gesture of hers, twining around and around her forefinger the gold chain she wore, sometimes pulling it so tight she seemed about to strangle herself. Then she said, "Marriage has its comforts too.

It makes you feel secure." She laughed out loud. "I suppose that's a very petty-bourgeois way of looking at it... Besides, I loved my husband, I always did. And not being married should create a slight degree of anxiety, don't you think? About what will happen today, tomorrow, later on." Had she ever felt that anxiety? he asked. "No, never. I was perfectly happy, perfectly at peace."

Mateus had wondered, at the time, what exactly she was getting at. Nothing, he realized later. For all her outward restlessness, she was at peace, as if that restlessness in a way preserved her peace. She was a fragile woman, but, by her side, he felt surrounded by the protective halo of near invulnerability that children feel when their mothers are close by. This was a new feeling and very pleasant, one he had never known as a child, because, right up until the end, his mother had been someone who was killing herself—who had perhaps already killed herself—working, but who at the same time was asking others, silently imploring them—especially him, her son—for help and compassion. Only once had she been strong, and he preferred not to remember that day.

However, he did remember it as he lay on the bed in the enchanted-palace-hotel of his childhood, and right in the center of that image was Graça—José Osório's wife and Ginho's mother. The small boy he had been that summer (and the previous spring and winter too) was always daydreaming about her. He would close his eyes and imagine her bending over him, stroking his hair, he could feel the kiss she would sometimes plant on his forehead, on his right temple. She was a real beauty, Graça. Tall, pale-complexioned, with wide, heavy-lidded green eyes. She wasn't skinny and anxious like his mother, nor internally serene and protective like Alberta. Whenever she was there, or if she simply passed by, she had a vital force that attracted all men's eyes; he could see this now in retrospect, although without being absolutely certain it was true. As if she were a beautiful magnet and they were mere iron filings. Any conversations lost their normal rhythm because, suddenly, everyone was simultaneously restless and entranced. People would look at each other, but very quickly, with eyes that alighted then left. Afterward—that is for the rest of his life—all the women he had known were poor imitations: false gold, fake jewels, cultured pearls at best. Mateus saw again her remarkable eyes, her small, straight nose, her delicate, tremulous nostrils, her smooth, thick dark hair, which she wore caught back at the nape of her neck. People would look at her, talk about her, but she didn't seem to notice, as if she existed in her own personal atmosphere, protected by an invisible glass dome. Mateus could still remember the vague smile she always wore, which may have meant only that she was happy to be alive and to be so beautiful.

When he rang the doorbell—a sort of small, ornate key that you turned to the right—she would sometimes open the door and ask him kindly if he'd come to see Ginho. He would nod timorously, and Graça would smooth his hair with her hand. "He's in his room, but don't stay too long, he has to study." Mateus would immediately do as he was told, even though he would have preferred to stay there, gazing at her. Seeing her seemed to him the very height of happiness.

One day, he'd seen something else, but, since he was only ten at the time (or perhaps eleven?) he hadn't thought it very important. It happened at the Café Flor do Mar, where he had gone for his usual free glass of water. She was sitting at the bar, and everyone was looking at her in the usual restless, entranced way. Graça, though, remained as still as a stone goddess, while one of her hands mechanically stirred a glass of lemonade in which floated a single ice cube. Then, at some point, someone came in. An equally beautiful man—how could he not have noticed this before?—and that man had smiled, and she had smiled, and Mateus had understood (not at that precise moment, but later, quite a lot later) that those two people were suddenly alone in the world, alone in the crowd. They must have had similar faces (and this he did think as he was holding his glass of iced water, even though he was distracted and had perhaps forgotten the terrible thirst of a moment ago): that of the *hero* who would vanquish the traitor, and the *girl* he would end up marrying. The *hero* in question, though, was his father—and this was the first time he had seen his father in the role of hero—and his father was, of course, married. The *girl* was also married, and they both had children. Such a story already went beyond his understanding, because he couldn't see how there could possibly be a suitably happy ending. Perhaps for that very reason he had thought no more about it, until the day he stopped outside the movie theater to look at the poster for a Western. Standing right next to him were two women talking. One of them, he remembered now, was the woman in the shawl he'd happened to pass that very morning, the one who had then disappeared into her house. The women were talking about Graça and his father, and in the most disgusting way too. At least, the little boy found it disgusting. One of them was saying, "It would be a kindness really to tell Senhor Osório what's going on. People are making fun of the poor man." The other woman agreed: "Yes, you're quite right." The little boy, Mateus, had moved slowly away, thinking: They'll tell him, and then he'll kill her. He didn't think, of this he was sure, he'll kill *him*, but he'll kill *her*. That's how it was in the movies he'd seen, and that's how it must be in real life. What could he do? He didn't know, and since he was only ten (or perhaps eleven), he decided to tell his mother. His mother would have to do something. For some mysterious reason he had forgotten the scene in the café and thought it was all a lie, a big lie, Mama. However, when she heard what he said, she turned deathly pale, as if she was about to collapse right there and then. "So everyone knows," she said. "Listen, don't say a word of this to anyone, not to your father or to Ginho. Not a word to Ginho."

That night there was a big scene, and a week later his mother left for Lisbon on the night train with him in tow. She had spent days packing their suitcases and packing everything up. The furniture was sold by mutual agreement.

It was twenty to eight when Mateus rang the bell—no longer a key you turned, but a button you pushed—at the house on Rua da Palmeira, which was right next door to the house that was, for the moment, still his. A short, skinny girl with stringy, shoulder-length, greenish-blonde hair opened the door and held out one small, firm hand, which he shook mechanically.

"I'm Natália," she said somewhat abruptly. "My mother's told me about you. So has Jorge."

"Ah, yes, Jorge. How is he?" he said equally abruptly, not really aware of what he was saying.

"I don't know. He's away at a conference about bones. Apparently, it's fascinating."

She showed him into a large room that had once been two rooms—both fairly large—furnished with colorful armchairs, soft rugs, a green-and-gold sideboard with, on top, a record player pouring forth a spiritual that stopped on a high note because someone suddenly turned off the machine, and bye-bye Ella Fitzgerald.

Mateus advanced hesitantly toward the mortal remains of Graça's beauty, which were smiling at him from beside the record player. A large lady with thin legs, who was squeezed, likely with some difficulty, into a polka-dot rayon dress. White polka dots on a cinnamon-brown background. Unexpectedly, her hair was the same color as her dress, and her eyes, though less green, were still green—still the large, oblique, heavy-lidded eyes of Graça.

"Well, if it isn't Matinho!" said her firm voice, her friendly, confident, steady voice, just as it used to be, a voice that never hesitated or stumbled. She smiled, then added with an amused look on her face, "My, how you've grown! You were only this high then, a little boy, and not very tall for your age either. You were nine, weren't you? How time flies! It seems like only yesterday."

"Well, I haven't grown that much," said Mateus, who wasn't particularly tall.

She paused to consider, probably searching out

lost images or trying to reconstruct others, worn thin by time. "People change so much, don't they? It's impossible to know how they'll turn out. You, for example… I was expecting some melancholy little fellow."

"That's me."

She laughed. "Not at all!" And she studied him more closely. "Only your eyes, perhaps, and something about your mouth are as I remember them… You've even managed to tame your hair. You're an entirely different person. But then so am I. We spend our lives dying and being reborn."

Mateus admired her for having plunged straight back into the old days, without the slightest hesitation. And so naturally too… Did she think he knew nothing about what had happened? That was, after all, possible. On her face, her old smile. Or was it simply because she had been beautiful? Because she had once been beautiful.

Graça had meanwhile returned to the present, and the present was this man, here in her house, who had come to supper, who must be offered a drink, and with whom she must make conversation. "But do sit down. What would you like to drink? Martini? Whiskey? I have vermouth too, if you like. José used to adore vermouth, but now, poor thing, he doesn't drink at all." When she spoke of her husband, she grew serious. "How did you find him?" she asked. "He's aged, hasn't he?" She didn't wait for his answer, which probably didn't much interest her anyway. What interested her were her own words and the fact that she had said them. As Mateus recalled and could now confirm, she was a woman who had always liked the sound of her own voice. There was even something sensual about the simplest, most trifling of her phrases—things said for the sake of saying them. She drew them out, savoring each word. "He *has* aged, well, that's only normal," she went on. "He should seek help, do something, but he doesn't want to. Like all men who used to be healthy, he's ashamed of being ill. That's old age for you, though, there's nothing to be done about it. And what about Natália?" she asked, gaily changing the subject.

He looked around, and since the Natália in question was absent, he merely nodded and said:

"She was the one who opened the door for me. And yet... I don't quite see... Who *is* Natália?"

Graça gave a little laugh, and her laugh really had aged. Failing to reach the heights of yesteryear, it tried to rise up, only to fall back, pausing halfway up the scale, where it either repeated itself or faltered, becoming more cackle than laugh. "Goodness!" she cried, then fell silent, staring into space before saying again, "How time flies," adding, "Of course, you never knew her, how could you? Whatever was I thinking? Natália was born after you and your mother left. One or two years later, possibly two, or more. Or was it less? Natália, Natália!" she called loudly, rather too loudly and enthusiastically. "Na-tá-li-a!"

Natália, meanwhile, didn't seem impressed by all that energy expended on her account, and took her time before making an appearance. Her voice could be heard far away, at the other end of the house. "Coming!" she called. Shortly afterward, she announced in a slightly drawling voice, "Just a moment, I won't be long." Then, finally, there she was standing in the doorway, saying, "Right, what's up?" During those three announcements and their respective intervals, Graça kept her eyes trained—too hard—on the open door, and the expression on her face was one of expectation and possibly also apprehension, but why?

All the while sipping his martini, Mateus was looking in the same direction, obliged to by the circumstances, because to look anywhere else at that moment would be almost offensive. And even before Natália actually appeared, he suddenly recalled—for some unknown reason, perhaps because of her green-tinged hair—a small mermaid from his childhood who appeared in a book with colored illustrations, a book that had been lost during one of their many house moves. But only because of her green hair, he thought. Otherwise, the daughter of the old mermaid sitting there before him now had nothing mythological about her at all, and could not have been less mermaid-like. Disheveled hair, unlovely face, creased pants (beneath which one could sense a pair of sturdy legs—thick calves and skinny thighs), and an over-large man's white shirt, possibly her brother's. She was still standing where, you might say, she had been washed up on the shore, leaning in the doorway, waiting. Graça, though, seemed to have forgotten why she had summoned her and simply looked at her daughter as if she had been there since the dawn of time, waiting to provide her with some answer or for her presence to fill that empty space.

"Do you know where your father is, what's keeping him?" she asked at last.

She had said what needed to be said, nothing

more was necessary. The man understood then that she was covering her tracks, and he instinctively lowered his eyes, as if embarrassed by the vague suspicion, the glimmer of a suspicion, that had surfaced inside him. "One or two years," she had said. "Perhaps more? Or perhaps less?" And now she had summoned Natália from the far end of the house, with her creased trousers and her vegetable-green hair, simply in order to say "your father" and for him, Mateus, to hear her say "your father." Which could also mean: "Careful, lips sealed, the girl doesn't know anything about that old story." Yes, it could also mean that. He, Mateus Silva, always hesitated a little before building certainties out of hypotheses. Not that this meant he didn't build them for his own use, just in case.

Natália slowly detached herself from the doorway and sloped into the room, where, bending slightly, she took a cigarette from a cigarette case and lit it; and Mateus noticed that she fumbled a little, seemed ill at ease, her gestures awkward—somehow not quite right. "Don't you smoke?" she asked without looking at him, or only glancingly. It was as if he was there, yes, and that she recognized the fact, but as if this was of no importance, as if his presence was so insignificant as to be barely noticeable, and that, at that moment, there were infinitely more important things to consider than his presence.

Mateus took a final sip of his now lukewarm martini and realized that Natália hadn't answered her mother's question, just as her mother appeared to have suddenly forgotten or to have lost all interest in being given an answer. Was this how they always were together? Did they understand each other so well that there was no point in completing what had been said or suggested or thought? Understood each other so well or so badly that silence was response enough?

Natália stubbed out her almost unsmoked cigarette, as meticulously and ferociously as if she loathed it (and Osório always chose his cigarettes with great care), and said she would call the factory, perhaps he was still there. That "he" seemed to Mateus to be a response to the "your father" of earlier on, but this may just have been his imagination. Graça thought this was a good idea, and she appeared relieved when Natália slouched out of the room. And yet, when she summoned Natália a few minutes earlier, Mateus had the feeling that Graça felt uncomfortable being alone with him.

"We heard about your father's death," she said suddenly, calmly, but in a very low voice. "I was very sad to hear that. Your father was a true friend. One finds so few true friends in life. Most so-called friends always want more from us, demanding our gratitude, and treating us as if we were just things or dogs. Devoted dogs, who must lick their master's hand. Your father was different."

Into Mateus's head came: "He didn't ask me to go with him, to leave my husband and my son, my home, to embrace the scandal and run away with him somewhere; he didn't ask me to exchange security for insecurity, an easy life for a difficult one." These words emerged out of nowhere, without him even having thought them, leaving him almost perplexed because such an idea had never occurred to him before.

"Your father was different," she said again.

Different from whom? From which other men? From how many others? Really? "Was he?"

"He was," she said very seriously, but it seemed to Mateus that in her eyes there was a particularly bright, alert look.

He would have liked to talk about his father, because he'd had so few opportunities in the past.

It had always been a taboo subject with his mother. And so he had continued to see him through the eyes of a child, the eyes of the Matinho who used to go racing down the streets in his Renault or kicking out at nothing at all. These were vague, imprecise recollections, occasionally besmirched by a very real, albeit figurative, stain, but he didn't feel brave enough to ask Graça anything. Also, he had a sense suddenly that she hadn't really known his father well and wouldn't be able to enlighten him in the way he wanted. He decided there and then that she was a stupid woman. She may know which side her bread is buttered on, but she really isn't very clever. She's an empty vessel. In the men who loved her, she had loved herself. But now that she's old… What will be left inside her now? A lot of flab, but what else?

"And how's Lisbon?"

"It's still there. Still the same."

"I would have liked to live in Lisbon, but it never happened. José was seriously considering it as a possibility, but then Ginho…" She failed to finish the sentence and began another. "He's at a conference, you know. About osteology."

"Yes, so I heard."

"Oh really? Who from?"

"Well, from Senhor Osório…and from your daughter."

"Ah."

A disconsolate, but not entirely discouraged "ah." After the conference, he would be coming here with his fiancée, because Ginho was going to be married—"Did you know that?" "No, I didn't"—to a delightful young woman from a very good family. One of the very best families. In October. It was all arranged. He'd sprung this on them only two months ago; he'd just turned up with his fiancée without a word of warning—typical Ginho.

"It must be said, though, that he couldn't have made a better choice. Rita is like a girl from another era. She's highly educated and nobody's fool, but so unassuming… She's a brilliant cook, a wonderful housewife. No one meeting her would ever know she's the daughter of Adérito Alves, the owner of CIPPAR, a regular captain of industry. You've probably heard of him…"

He nodded.

"Her mother, Dona Alice, is terribly refined, her name's always in the newspapers, you must have seen it. Charity balls, things like that. And *so* kind.

Oh, yes, they're excellent people. I was always afraid Ginho would be snapped up by some shrewd little operator, if you know what I mean, or by some pretty, empty-headed little fool."

Or, as was clear, by some empty-pocketed little fool. He had this thought at the very moment he caught Natália's faint smile, for she had returned—when?—and was perched on the arm of a chair. What was she smiling at? At her mother's enthusiasm for that daughter-in-law, who would, in a way, help them rise up the social ladder, thanks to that very refined mother of hers? Or was she laughing at him, Mateus, and at his sad or disconsolate expression, which he had perhaps failed to disguise? Because Mateus was listening to Graça and thinking, not about the house that would probably be demolished, or about Adérito's daughter, but about a beautiful woman sitting in the midst of all those people in the Café Flor do Mar and looking at his father, smiling at him as if no one else in the world existed.

"Jorge is our pride and joy," said Natália, still smiling.

Her mother winced, then pretended to be amused, before asking abruptly:

"Did you call your father?"

"He's on his way. He left the factory a little while ago and should arrive at any moment. Should I ask them to serve supper?"

"Yes, do."

When Natália left, Graça asked, "And what about your mother?"

"She died shortly after my father died."

"Oh, I didn't know that. I'm terribly sorry."

Where had he heard those same words spoken in the same tone of voice, at once caring and indifferent? Ah yes, it had been that very morning, José Osório saying that he didn't know and was terribly sorry. However, she immediately changed the subject. Willfully or aggressively. She paused at the end of the last subject, like someone planting her feet firmly on the ground and refusing to go any farther, which is exactly what she did. She planted her small, plump, possibly swollen feet firmly on the ground and looked around for an alternative direction to take, then talked instead about supper. Did Mateus like roast chicken? That's what they were having anyway, nothing fancy…

José Osório arrived at that point, apologizing profusely, and saving her from saying anything more on culinary matters. They sat down at the table right away. The old dining room hadn't changed much, apart from there being more silverware. The factory really must be taking care of itself, and very good care too, as Osório had said that morning. The old provincial family, with little money of its own, was now, he could see, a wealthy family, with houses, a flourishing factory, a son practicing medicine in Lisbon, a daughter-in-law who was the child of the owner of a big company, a man who doubtlessly ruled over a few hundred employees, a man who didn't need to bend the knee to anyone really, or only enough to prove himself a patriot and part of a flourishing social class. All of this, of course, would be done discreetly, because it was best not to burn one's bridges.

The table was immaculately laid, and the maid wore a neat, pleated apron. Natália was sitting on the other side of the table, smiling quietly. Separating them was a small ship vase filled with flowers, a silver ship of course. She had inherited from her mother the absentminded smile that flickered across her face. Her mother's smile, though, was a happy smile. Because she was beautiful. Because she had been beautiful. And loved too. Because she had a remarkable son. Because she was going to have a daughter-in-law who came from one of Lisbon's wealthiest families. Because, years ago, she *hadn't* ruined her life. For all those reasons, all of which were right. Natália's smile was a secret smile, one that was born deep inside her, although the foam from that smile was visible. The light, brief foam of a smile. Was she laughing at her mother? At their visitor? At her father, José Osório? At the maid? Or the chicken, which really was delicious, "It's really delicious, Dona Graça," someone said.

He regretted having come. Which is why he welcomed with open arms the subject offered him by Osório—, namely dried figs, the industry to which he had dedicated his whole life, and which, according to him, was currently undergoing a crisis. And yet, that very morning, he had said that the factory was taking care of itself. And the house and the family, apart from Natália, had a decidedly prosperous air. And Dona Graça's fingers glittered with rings.

After supper, coffee was served in the living room, and Graça returned to the subject of Ginho, who had his practice in the most fashionable part of Lisbon. "Drop in on him some day, he'd love to see you."

At some point, Natália had vanished without a word. And neither her father nor her mother appeared to notice her absence.

The night was long and hot, as if it needed to pause now and then from sheer exhaustion. Mateus spent it either staring at the little points of light on the sea or, with the bedside lamp on, reading the newspaper he'd bought from the girl at the newsstand on his way back to the hotel. "So, you managed to find Rua da Palmeira?" "Yes, I did, thank you." "And the palm tree?" "The palm tree?" "Yes, it's still there. Didn't you notice? I asked around this afternoon. Apparently, there was an incident there a few days ago, with firemen and an articulated ladder and everything, and all because of a cat."

During that sleepless night, he also thought a lot about Graça past and present. Time provides a perfect substitute for death, and is even crueler. Death perpetuates, time destroys. Or rather it delivers the coup de grâce—and how. He found it very hard to recall the young Graça, as if the present-day Graça had completely doused that earlier luminous image, spattering it with mediocrity, drowning it in trite, homely, utilitarian words and ideas.

And Natália? Was she his sister? The whole time he had spent with her, he had searched her face, her ideas, for something familiar, but had seen nothing of himself or of his father. Besides, how could he have, given that he could scarcely remember his father, and his mother had conscientiously torn up any photos of him? Natália was a stranger, and, what's more, she clearly wanted to be a stranger. She had barely spoken, and had only looked at him furtively, and, in the end, had left without a word. Before that, it's true, she had smiled, but hers was an uncomfortable, slightly mocking smile, on the hunt for something risible, and only smiling when she found it. Over supper, she had remained completely silent and had vanished immediately after coffee.

Mateus had stayed for a while longer, mainly out of inertia, and because he thought it would be rude to leave at once. Graça had turned on a small electric fan, which made the room very comfortable. José Osório had launched into a monologue about how business wasn't going—*wasn't* going?—well.

It was midnight by the time Mateus managed to make his exit. The three of them were standing in the middle of the room talking about Ginho when Osório said that while they were talking about other things, he'd been pondering what to do with the house, and wondered if it might be best to leave doing any work on the house until next spring.

Graça cried, "That's a long time!" and he explained that getting building licenses from the council always took ages. Besides, there was another possibility: demolish both houses and build a larger one that would bring in some money. They could keep two floors for themselves and the children, and rent out the other floors as furnished accommodations. It was something to think about, given all the foreign tourists…

"Don't you agree?" he asked his wife.

"Hm, yes…" she murmured dreamily at the thought of this fascinating new possibility.

Mateus had said goodbye to the lady of the house, and was about to say to her husband, "See you tomorrow." He, however, had picked up his hat. "I'll walk a little way with you. I could do with a breath of air."

He went with him almost as far as the newsstand and spoke, among other things, about Graça, quite casually as if Mateus knew everything—well, didn't he? "How did she seem? She's aged a lot, hasn't she?" And there was on his face a vaguely anxious expression. "Old would you say?"

"No, no. There are some women you could never say were exactly…"

Osório interrupted him. "No, no, she's old all right, and just as well really. Do you remember how pretty she was?"

"Very pretty. The most beautiful woman I…"

"Ah, so you do remember. And you were just a little boy then… She really was stunning, and I made the biggest mistake of my life marrying her. I regretted it of course, but now I think I did the right thing.

Now, that is. Times change and so do our ideas. I've never been one to worry about what happened in the past. If anyone was to blame, it was me, not her. She was a beauty, and I was a silly old fool. I always was. I was determined to get married, and I chose a wife other men couldn't take their eyes off."

He paused, then said, "One day, she started putting on weight, her feet swelled up, and her hair started to go gray. Did she make a big drama out of it though? No, she just accepted it. And suddenly, everything calmed down. I've even come to think that she…that everything that happened… But it's the now that matters. She began to care more about things like the house, money, the future. To take an interest in my problems…"

"I understand." In Ginho's problems, in Natália's, perhaps in her own too. *After the pleasures of the flesh, the pleasures of the table*, but he couldn't say this to Osório, who must already know, after all, he wasn't stupid.

"Anyway, see you tomorrow," Osório said, holding out his hand. "The notary's office is right next to the Café Flor do Mar. You remember where it is, don't you?" he asked again.

Mateus remembered perfectly.

He walked a few steps, and went to the newsstand to buy a paper. "So you managed to find Rua da Palmeira?"

Now he was on a different train, or perhaps the same one, but traveling in the opposite direction, leaving behind, this time forever, these trees, houses, and stations. He felt tired, and, for the first time in his difficult life, he felt poor, wretchedly poor, despite the check he had in his wallet. For now he had nothing he could call his own. The people around him seemed far too close, almost aggressively present. Completely at ease, at home you might say, cozily ensconced in their invisible worlds, which touched and even bruised his own small, modest world. There was a burly man, probably Dutch—reading a newspaper so thick it resembled a huge puff pastry tart— and who, at regular intervals, would blow cigar smoke in his face. A blonde, pink-cheeked German woman. An old English woman, wearing a white hat adorned with flowers, so very English and so very old that she was reading *Pride and Prejudice*. A middle-aged couple, this time Portuguese, who didn't exchange a single word throughout the whole journey, as if they had long since said everything there was to say. The *gnädige Frau* would smile now and then like a person pleased with herself and everyone else. She smiled, this *Constanze*, at the landscape, and at the watch she occasionally consulted.

He found himself thinking about Alberta, and he did so objectively, more in order to pass the time than out of any desire or need to think about her. To begin with, he saw her sitting curled up in her blue-and-gray armchair (gray fans on blue fans or vice versa), turned aggressively in on herself, legs and feet included, her transparent conch-like hands clamped over her ears. This was Alberta now. When he had first met her, she was different. A plump woman, the kind who eats almost nothing, gets up early, works all day, somewhat shambolically, at keeping the house clean and tidy, but still never loses weight and never complains. It's as if women like Alberta had an engine constantly running inside them. And if they do sit down for a moment in between two tasks, they talk and talk… She was also one of those women who can't bear to live on their own, but who often end up completely alone because of their inability to put on a brave face. "You were born an ant," he would sometimes tell her when he saw her bustling about the house. She would shrug: "Ants have lots of children. I mean, have you seen the size of the average anthill? In that respect, I've never been an ant, and in other respects too. Have you ever seen an ant without plenty of food stored away for the coming winter? No, I'm no ant. I would love to be a cricket. Or a migratory bird. Or an eel on its way to the Sargasso Sea. Something like that." Mateus had been living in her house for two years, and for the last six months, Alberta really hadn't been herself. She had lost weight, was less talkative, moved very slowly, had pains she couldn't quite locate—in her stomach, she said. She went to the doctor and had various tests. The doctor asked if she had any family. "I have a gentleman friend," she had said. And she must have blushed when she said that. "Tell him to call me. You need someone to look after you." The following day, he had gone to the consulting room and was seen immediately. The doctor asked him to sit down, then pronounced the word he most feared. "So, there's no hope?" The doctor said, "We could operate, of course, but... Besides, she said categorically that she doesn't want an operation." "Did you tell her what was wrong, Doctor?" "Of course not, but I'm sure she knows. I'm also sure she'll pretend until the bitter end that she doesn't. Do what you can to help her. And call me whenever you need to. I've prescribed some pills and some injections. Make sure she takes them. And that's all we can do for now."

What was Alberta thinking about as she sat curled up in the gray-and-blue armchair? She didn't say much. She didn't complain, not about her illness. Mateus sometimes saw a pained expression on her face, but then she would go and find her pills. She would talk, but not about the things she used to talk about. And in a bitter tone of voice too. About what she hadn't done and suddenly regretted not having done. This, for example: Never having learned to swim; never having owned an emerald ring; never having seen the Acropolis.

Which is why Mateus had sold his parents' house, not to save Alberta—would he have done that to save her were such a thing possible?—but so that she could go and see the Acropolis. Not that she had wanted him to sell the house, but neither did she want to die without having seen those ruins. She didn't want to just stay there, in the apartment where she had always lived (and possibly been happy), waiting for the end. She sometimes launched into strange, unexpected monologues. First, it was the emerald ring. A ring, how odd. They were sitting next to the radio one night, after supper. She had taken her medicine shortly before and seemed to be feeling well. Then she said:

"You know that ring I dreamed about all my life, even if I hated the dream? Well, I think I inherited it, the dream I mean, from my mother, even though the ring-she-never-had was different. I even began to save up for it. But then it stopped being part of my dreams, because I stopped having dreams. Or only occasionally the Acropolis dream… Anyway, I'm not saying I don't miss them, especially on nights when I can't sleep. The old time for lullabies and fairy tales. The time for love. I toss and turn, but I can't find anything interesting to focus on even for a few minutes. Nothing. A complete blank. Do you understand?"

"Well…" he said hesitantly.

"No, you don't understand," she said firmly. Then with a shrug, she added, "I really did miss them, but why did they disappear? Why? Why? I close my eyes, and my mouth is pressed up against a cold wall. Dreaming about what? Hoping for what? The wall must be damp from my breath. Sometimes I'm afraid of falling asleep. Do you know what it's like to feel afraid of falling asleep?" She waited then for his answer as if many things depended on it. "No, you can't know that either. It's too subjective. No, not subjective, something you have to experience yourself." She laughed a wry little laugh and added, "It's a shame I never showed any interest in other people's lives, because apparently that helps a lot." A devastating tinkle of bracelets, three of them, round and identical, slave bracelets she called them. Once there had been five or seven or eleven. She grew serious. "I wish I'd done things I didn't do. I've told you that before, haven't I? For example, I wish I'd studied medicine, because I really think that was the one thing I seriously wanted to do. But I refused point-blank to go to medical school, can you understand that? As if my destiny had already been decided. Do you believe in destiny?"

"No, and neither do you, Alberta."

"No, I don't. Anyway, I also wish I could speak a secret language, the kind no one else learns, a kind of luxury. Japanese or Farsi, or Creole, that would be ideal. Languages of no immediate use, that aren't a way of earning money. Another thing would be contact lenses, because I've always looked hideous in glasses. I'd also like…"

"What?" he asked as if she had suddenly become a child.

"To see this out to the end with a certain simplicity. That might be possible. We're all slowly evolving inside, and when I say 'inside' I mean inside."

That had been the night he suggested she make that journey. The emerald ring struck him as too stupid, but the trip to the Acropolis, which she'd seen for the first time in a school history book when she was fifteen… On the left-hand page, she was sure of it. And down one slope flowed the spring of Klepsydra…

"Klepsydra? Are you sure?"

"Yes, I'm sure it was Klepsydra."

"And what is this Klepsydra spring?"

"I don't know."

On the eve of his departure, she seemed to understand the pointlessness of it all. And yet she hadn't asked him not to sell the house, hadn't once again asked him not to sell it. She had talked a lot that day, and her thoughts, liberated by the idea of that future trip, seemed to fix only on death, as if the journey would happen afterward, once she'd rested from dying. On death, its origins, its effects and long- or short-term consequences. The most immediate consequence, of course, was where she would be buried. In the earth. She had even said, "No cabinets, no drawers, I've always hated them, as you well know."

He advised her to put aside such morbid thoughts. Alberta, though, would not be silenced. "So many things get forgotten at the back of a drawer… We never pull them all the way out, you see. There's always something stuck a few inches from the back. Forgotten and, in a way, protected. Only in a way, though. No, that would be horrible. In the earth there's always hope." She hadn't explained further, but he knew she was referring to what Lavoisier said: "Nothing is born, nothing dies." Far better to help a weed flourish than to provide a simple feast for the usual suspects. She began to ramble a little then. "What will happen to them when there's nothing left? When there's no more food? You don't know? Well, it is a subject of general interest. There must be a bibliography about it. When you think of all the pedants and nerds out there, and yet…"

She seemed like someone half-drunk. Drunk

on death. Giddy, almost falling over. An egotist, her of all people, who always gave everything and asked for nothing in return. Her soft voice had grown harsh, hard and bitter. She knew she was going to die, although she never actually said the word. She knew that Mateus was going to sell the house so that she could make that stupid journey *before*—the only ridiculous action in her whole sensible existence. Would she come back? Would she stay there? It was as if she were having her revenge, but on what, on whom?

Mateus put down his suitcase and turned the key in the lock. "Is that you?"

He went straight to her room and sat down on the edge of the bed. She folded him in her scrawny white arms, and seemed quite like the old Alberta. Or perhaps not, perhaps she simply resembled a drowning woman whose greatest fear is that her rescuer will let her go, grow weary of carrying her weight and cast her someplace where there'll be no firm ground beneath her feet and nothing to hold on to.

Alberta gave him a long look and smiled wanly—for hers was now a poor excuse for a smile—before telling him that he shouldn't have done it. Then, slightly embarrassed, she went on to ask if *it* had been a great shock to him. And she repeated her *leitmotiv*: "My poor Mateus, was it really necessary? No, of course it wasn't. A mere whim. Your problem is that you love me."

Ah, there she was wrong, he thought, running his hand over her dry, drab hair. He didn't love her, not enough to give her everything he had at least: house and memories. However, he'd had no option. She was, for all intents and purposes, his wife, someone who, like him, had no one else in the world. The wife who would sometimes ask him anxiously if he wasn't already fed up with her. He smiled, and kissed her lightly on the corner of her mouth. "How have you been? Did the cleaning lady come?"

"Yes, she did. And Luísa came yesterday. She brought some cakes, made tea, and we chatted for a while."

"What about?" he asked, not that he particularly cared.

"Oh, this and that, I can't honestly remember. Among other things, she talked about some face cream we used when we were girls; she said very seriously that it no longer works, that she still uses it but it doesn't have the same effect. How very Luísa! And she said it so seriously, so earnestly. Poor Luísa! Or should I say lucky Luísa?"

She fell silent. Then she returned to the main road from which she had deviated. "It's all my fault! I shouldn't cause you problems, but I do nothing else. That's how it is, though. My husband…"

"Leave your husband out of it."

She, however, would not be stopped: "Can you ever forgive me? I don't mean now, but later? I know I'm only going to spend some of the money, but… That house was very important to you, a kind of treasure chest. A sealed chest with no key. I've made you pay an exorbitant price."

"You didn't ask me to do anything, Alberta," he said gently.

"It's as if I had though. I let you do it. I wonder if I didn't actually suggest that you sell the house. Unconsciously, I mean. Something along the lines of, 'If I had anything worth selling, I'd go and see the Acropolis.' But I swear that if I did, I wasn't thinking about your house, just that if *I* had something to sell… You do believe me, don't you, Mateus? Tell me you do."

"I believe you. But why torment yourself like this?"

"I've done a lot of thinking these last two days. Except when Luísa was here. I thought, for example, that perhaps we were too hasty. You could have taken out a mortgage…"

"I couldn't afford to pay it, Alberta."

"Ah, of course."

"I had supper at their house, you know."

"Really? I assumed that…well, that you wouldn't be on exactly friendly terms with them."

"It was a business dinner. Businessmen often lunch or dine together. It's usually the one who's made the best deal, in this case Osório, who pays for the meal."

"You should know."

"It's not a question of knowing or not. As I said, they came to me. I wrote to the notary, and they turned up."

"Yes," she said, slightly put out. "Of course…" Then, in order to distance herself a little from her problem and from further distasteful details about money, to avoid them as much as possible, she asked about Graça, was she old now?

Mateus said: "Yes…" But then he hesitated, leaned against the bedframe, and slightly closed his eyes. "Old isn't really the right word," he said cautiously. "Her former beauty, well, that's long gone, but there's still something that will perhaps always be there. Her husband isn't aware of it, and she herself may not be either. There are some women one could never dismiss as old, and she must be one of them," he said, finally completing the sentence he'd begun in his brief conversation with Osório that night, as they walked down the road. And he went on: "There are her green eyes, for example, and her voice, both of which have stayed almost the same in the midst of all that physical and emotional ruin."

"I've never known anyone like that," said Alberta, flinching a little, the pain as yet only slight.

"Perhaps I'm not explaining it very well. Besides, it's not important."

"No," she said, agreeing.

"When are you going to sort out your passport?" Mateus asked. "Tomorrow?"

"I might feel more up to it on Monday."

"Do you want me to…"

"No, no. I'm the one making the journey after all? So…"

Alberta suddenly leaned against his shoulder. She emerged from the sheets like a snail coming out of its shell, and there was something oddly invertebrate about her body. "I'm going to suffer horribly," she said with a serenity undermined by the tremor in her voice. "I don't know when or how. Will I have the strength to come back, Mateus? No, I'm not going to cry because that's not like me, but I am going to suffer horribly when I'm alone on the plane. What will I think about? How will I pass the time? Do you think I'll come back, Mateus?"

"Look, it's up to you if you go or not, but of course you'll come back. It'll all be fine. You'll be making the journey you've wanted to make for years, and it'll be great, you'll see. You can trust me, you can count on me. Sometimes we men…"

She broke in: "Speak in the singular, please. Talk about you, I don't care about other men. Plurals terrify me, I find crowds threatening, frightening. But there I am being selfish again," she said with a certainty that was clearly an act. "You've sacrificed everything you had for me, and here I am just talking about me me me. But then I always talk too much, don't I? I go on about superficial things and forget about other deeper subjects. You're not like that."

"Possibly," he said.

"It's true. You're not."

"No, I don't think I am, but I can't be sure." He was talking, but he was already somewhere else, where he didn't quite know, on his way to a future he could still not see clearly. It was only his body that was gazing at her tenderly through the windows of his eyes, stroking her dull hair, kissing her. It wasn't him. The body of a man alone in the world, a body without a soul, pure body.

On Monday morning, he went to cash the check and open an account. "Have you come into money, my friend?" asked the clerk, who knew him.

"I've just sold a house back home. I have a few debts to pay…"

"Was it a good house?"

"A house worth eighty *contos*."

"You're lucky to have something to sell," said the clerk phlegmatically.

Mateus agreed.

Thanks to the ears that Adérito Alves hired by the month or as a form of overtime purely in order to listen, he soon found out that Mateus had arrived late that day, and he stopped by his desk to ask, in that replete voice of his—devoid of empty spaces or obstacles, an inner world from which it emerged definitive and powerful—the reason for his late arrival. Mateus said that no one had woken him. "Goodness!" exclaimed the voice. "Do you still need someone to wake you up? At your age, man? I call that either a case of extreme forgetfulness or not having enough to think about." Everyone laughed, furtively, like discreet embarrassed courtiers, and Mateus found himself smiling, a reflex reaction that caught him unawares and that tugged at the corners of his mouth and refused to leave. Meanwhile he was thinking, I sold a house. A house where that girl-from-another-era could spend the summer vacation with her husband. I sold it too cheaply, almost gave it away, don't I deserve to be half an hour late? No, he didn't. How ridiculous, he was getting Ginho's fiancée slightly muddled up with Alves' daughter. "It's not good enough, Silva," said the boss pompously and loudly enough for everyone to hear and enjoy. "It's not good enough, Silva (*he* was Silva). One thing I've always insisted on is punctuality. I hope it doesn't happen again," he declared, having already turned his back and set off toward another desk, where a typist immediately began typing much faster, hurling herself vertiginously along the next line, pausing only momentarily at the margin. Adérito stopped briefly, looked, then continued on. The typist slackened her speed. The frosted glass door opened and closed on that powerful man. "A regular captain of industry. You've probably heard of him."

Elsa, who occupied the desk opposite his, took her compact out of her handbag, primped her hair in the mirror, then lit a cigarette and smiled at Mateus. She was about the same age as him, a widow, who tended to be rather overly made-up, and with whom he enjoyed chatting a little. Everyone liked her, and called her "the merry widow." Elsa knew this, but didn't care. One day, she had said to Mateus that Adérito was a man who gave off no energy at all. "It's true," she had added. "Everybody gives off a vitality that can sometimes be felt by those close by. No, not vitality exactly, a kind of vital force, which can be either attractive or repellent. The vehicle for that force could be their eyes, their voice, their gestures, even their complexion or their smile... Not with Adérito though. He's a rock with the power of movement and speech, but inside he's just a rock. Like that one over there. A solid mass. Do you think he ever reads a novel? I doubt it. He's the kind of person who goes to the movies with his family, but only to those movie-houses with comfortable seats, and once there, he immediately falls asleep, with Sofia Loren up there on the screen. He has no imagination at all. For him, Sofia Loren is never a woman, just a series of photographs in motion. I know what I'm talking about. A few days ago, I sat only a few seats away, and he was actually snoring."

That morning, she said to Mateus, "He can call it what he likes: order, good organization, paternalism, whatever. Basically, it's fear, a terrible fear that someone will rob him of ten minutes' working time.

Did you see how that girl over there started typing really fast? All right, she may not be very bright, but she knows that's what it's about. And his fear doesn't stop there. I realized this the day I saw him and his wife at the movies. She resembles a large white whale, and they say she looked like that even when they got married. And then there's a fear of death. Haven't you ever noticed that sometimes, when he's talking to us, he's also taking his pulse?"

"You're very observant!"

"You don't think I'm just a horrible gossip, do you?"

"No, not at all."

"Because if you do, you're quite wrong, Mateus. I'm no gossip, I'm not even particularly inquisitive. It's just that there are certain unbearable creatures I have to put up with, and that somehow unleashes in me…"

"I understand," he said.

She gave him a long look and smiled, as if that word "understand" had some hidden meaning. Or as if he, Mateus Silva, had clearly never understood anything, absolutely nothing.

At lunchtime, as he was leaving the building, he saw her leaning in the doorway. She still had the same disheveled, greenish hair, but instead of those crumpled trousers, she was wearing a blue linen skirt, a sleeveless black top, and a bag slung across her shoulders. Mateus began walking in her direction, but deliberately slowly, because he wasn't entirely sure it was her; it could, after all, be someone who looked a lot like her. Natália was probably where he had left her two days earlier. She had disappeared then without saying goodbye, so why would she come looking for him now? How could she have known where he was working if he hadn't told her? Why would Natália seek him out? She might be there for some completely different reason. It was even possible that she'd come there to speak to Adérito, and this was just an unfortunate coincidence. It was best to pretend he hadn't seen her.

Instead of walking directly toward her, he took a slightly curving route, one that would allow him to pass her at a sufficient distance that, if he kept looking straight ahead, he wouldn't catch her eye. Adopting an attentive gaze, as if intrigued or occupied with something going on out in the street, he quickened his pace. She, however, stepped forward and intercepted him, grabbing his arm with one small, firm hand. "Are you running away from me?" she asked, smiling.

Mateus pretended to be surprised. "What are you doing here? When did you arrive?"

"I didn't arrive. I live here. I just happened to have gone home for a few days. Or perhaps I didn't just happen to go home, I had my reasons. I needed money, and wrote them a letter asking for some. They suggested I go and see them so that we could talk."

"And did you talk?"

"No, but they gave me some money."

She fell silent. So did he. She still hadn't said anything that proved she'd come looking for him. On the other hand, she seemed to find it perfectly natural to meet him there.

"Are you headed somewhere?" she asked suddenly. "Now I mean."

"I'm going to have lunch."

"At home?"

"No."

"With someone else?"

"No."

"Can I have lunch with you? I need to talk to you, which is why I came looking for you."

"How did you know I worked here?"

She shrugged. "Call it intuition, if you like. Can I have lunch with you?"

Of course she could. Intuition, eh? And did she have something important to say to him?

She walked slowly along beside him, placing her feet one in front of another, on the cracks in the paving stones or between the cobbles in the street. Seen in profile, she wasn't ugly at all, there was even something rather charming about her. Her features were small and neat, she had quite high cheekbones, and at each corner of her mouth, a small comma-like line, which was there even when she was serious and silent. The line of someone who laughs a lot, though she didn't appear to be the type. They walked on a little, and she said:

"I don't know yet, it's too early to say. It might be important, and it might not. To be honest, I don't even know if I have anything to say to you. Anything worthwhile that is. Imagine (and she looked at him hard), imagine I have nothing to say and that I only came to see you because I suddenly felt like talking to you. Do you believe that?"

"No," he said. "I don't."

"Of course, why would you?" she answered—or asked—abruptly, and again she shrugged, clearly a tic of hers.

"Besides…" Mateus said.

"Besides what?"

"…you didn't strike me as being very talkative, *there*, as you put it."

"I'm not, and I'm not even a very good listener. Just an average listener, with highs and lows. Sometimes, though, even untalkative people like to tell their tale."

"Please do, I'm all ears."

"There's time for that. Anyway, I didn't say I had a tale to tell *you*, not at all."

They remained silent until they reached the café where he had lunch every day because it was near the office and cheap. She had resumed her search for the straight lines, intercepted at regular intervals by other shorter lines, on which to place her feet. Once they were seated, Natália said:

"I called you yesterday. Before coming to Lisbon, I got your address and number from the notary, and I called. If I'd been within striking distance, the woman who answered would have scratched my eyes out. Is she always like that?"

She appeared to ask this purely for the sake of asking, and clearly had no interest in the answer that would follow, that might follow. Mateus, however, sat there stiff and silent. He didn't respond, and then she started laughing as if the whole situation were terribly funny, and laughter was the natural consequence of what had been said or thought. There was something strange or different about her laugh; where did that laugh come from? Mateus traveled through time and space, straight back to the past—which was no longer so very easy—in search of Graça's laugh. But this laugh had nothing in common with hers, which had always been free and easy, always discreet. Natália's laughter seemed suddenly exaggerated, out of all proportion with the situation. But what was Natália laughing about? What?

"I just wanted to know where I could find you,

that's all," she said once she'd stopped laughing, "but that creature…"

She said "creature" in the same placid, indifferent tone in which she might have said "that charming lady who answered the phone." As if "creature" and "charming lady" were both equally natural and possible terms, as if it all depended on which card you were dealt. He had been dealt the Queen of Spades, well…it *is* a game of chance. It didn't matter. Next time one can always discard some cards and take new ones from the pack.

Not that Mateus reacted. He merely said, "She's very ill."

"That's no reason, is it? What does that have to do with me?"

"Nothing, of course."

"I hope I didn't offend her by saying that I needed to talk to you. Anyway, she didn't give you the message, because you clearly weren't expecting me. She did finally tell me where you worked, but obviously didn't say anything to you."

"She probably forgot."

She shrugged, then ate some of her omelet, took a sip of beer, and grimaced: "It's warm." Then, finally, she looked at Mateus. She was preparing to dive from the top of the cliff, entering the water, arms outstretched, in classic high-dive style. Mateus was perhaps hoping she might change her mind at the very last moment, but she didn't. Natália spoke without hesitation, although her eyes, which had abandoned their support, did wander a little away from his face, as if that face had suddenly become transparent.

"Above all, don't go thinking I'm your sister. I was born in 1942, by which time your father was long gone. I have a defect in my toes, like Jorge and like my father. The big toe and the one next to it are the same size. These family characteristics can be very useful sometimes, everyone should have them. How is it that God, or Nature, or whoever the relevant authority is, whether abstract or real, failed to think of that? Society could only gain by it, don't you think? It would be far more useful than all those sermons about virtue and hellfire. Do you believe in hell?"

"Well…"

"No, you don't. Well, I firmly believe that it does exist, although the devils seem to me far too literary and too Germanic. The hell I believe in is one with no devils, if you see what I mean. A hell with nothing and no one. Not even hell itself. Total isolation, with us banging our heads against nonexistent walls. Eternal isolation, for ever and ever, Amen. Complete incommunicability. Only the memory of words, gestures, images, and around us, no words, no gestures, no images. That's my idea of hell. Very literary, eh?"

"Or possibly delightful?" he asked.

"I confess I would be disappointed if…well, I think we should all pay for our mistakes. And I don't mean bureaucratic expressions of regret, with all the necessary paperwork in place. A few prayers for forgiveness and hurrah for salvation!"

"I've never been exactly mystical," he said, "but I am sort of a believer."

"I can tell that by looking at you."

"Really?"

"Really." A silence fell, then she said, "I'm very fond of my father. Before I found out, I thought him coarse and ignorant, although clever too. Afterward, I saw him through a different lens. I saw him for what he is. A businessman who buys houses at half their real price from people who aren't businessmen. Fine. But a businessman in every sense, one who doesn't let go of a good deal—what he considers to be a good deal—even if others think it disastrous. He rolls up his sleeves, fights, and doesn't give a damn about what other people think. And I don't think he's ever believed in monopolies."

"He talked to me about that a few days ago. That's not quite what he said, but more or less."

"Did he ever have any regrets?" she asked without looking at him.

"I believe so, but now he's happy."

"Good. I'm pleased to hear it."

They had finished lunch. Natália lit a cigarette. She spoke vaguely about her hometown, about how pleasant it was there in the summer. He asked her if there was still a movie theater on Rua de São Paulo Estreita. She told him about an American singer-songwriter who lived there, then the conversation took another direction, and Mateus found himself telling her that her mother had been the most beautiful woman he'd ever seen. Natália said, "Really?" Then looked at her watch.

It was getting late. She insisted on paying for her own lunch, ordered a coffee, and left.

Hours later, he left the office and went home. At his side was Natália, who he preferred not to think about. Only a part of Natália. Not her, of course, but a sensation in which there was not even a wisp of her green hair, a glow of her white face, an echo, however faint, of her voice. Still Natália though.

When he opened the door, he couldn't hear a sound, and he had the sense then of entering an empty house, as he had days before. A dead house. A foretaste of an ending anyway. When she left never to return (or to return only for a while, after all, what was she really thinking, did she even have a plan?), he probably couldn't stay there. He might pack his bags and go to a cheap hotel while he waited for her arrival or for her definitive absence. And then he would go back to the small ads: "Respectable gentleman…" He had forgotten about that particular quality of his, he must keep that in mind, it was useful. Respectability.

He walked down the corridor to Alberta's room. She was lying in bed, as she nearly always was at that hour, and she smiled at him. Then she spoke in a voice that struggled to be the same as it always had been, but that succeeded only in being totally different. The voice of someone in a large hall, standing before a huge audience, who desperately wants to appear to be at ease.

"My passport will be here in a few days. I'll be able to leave at the end of next week." She was twining a piece of thread around her right index finger, and at the base of her now scrawny neck there was a deep red mark, like the mark on a hanged man's neck when the rope broke too soon, except that the hanged man still won't be saved, he'll just be hanged again.

"I simply have to choose a date," she said. "I'll perhaps think about that tomorrow."

"Why tomorrow? Why not today or the day after tomorrow, Alberta?"

"I don't know, I really don't. I must be a bit confused, so pay no attention. Now that it's all arranged, now that you've sold the house, I keep asking myself…"

He didn't want to know what she'd been asking herself, and pretended to be distracted, looking around. "Do you want anything to eat?" he asked.

"No, the cleaning lady brought me some supper before she left. I think I'll read for a while. Luísa lent me some books. I've just started *War and Peace*. Have you read it?"

He said he had, thinking to himself that she would never finish it.

"Do you reckon I'll like it?" Alberta asked.

"I think it's an extraordinary book, but I don't know if you'll like it."

"Are you going to have some supper?"

"No, I'm going to do a bit of work first."

He left, closing the door behind him, and felt annoyed with himself for not feeling her suffering as much as he should. On the contrary, her suffering barely touched him, it was as if Alberta had gradually been moving further and further away from him, or he from her, and from where he was, he could barely see or feel her problems. "Out of sight, out of mind," his mother used to say about things that had happened in the past, and that he had forgotten.

Separated from Alberta now—by just a few feet—he saw clearly that he had never loved her, and that selling his house had been a mere gesture, a grand, secret gesture that had made him feel better about himself, unlike other gestures in the past, which had been rather less noble. Yes, he had sold the house and the memories it contained in order to feel that he was someone, that he was a man. Pure vanity. Meanwhile, she knew she was going to die, at least she certainly knew that today. Mateus had sensed the certainty in her, even though she hadn't—as she had on other occasions—said anything to make him think that.

"May I come in, Mateus?"

"Is that you?"

Who else would it be? He made a point of rustling the papers he sometimes brought home with him in order to finish some urgent job—he was a conscientious worker—then went over to the door, which, for no reason, out of pure habit, he always locked. She said again, "May I come in?"

He opened the door. "Why didn't you call me, Alberta? Sit down, sit down."

She sat down and gave him a long look. Finally, she said that when she died…

He interrupted her. "Don't be so morbid. That's what I call having an unhealthy mindset."

"Do you think so?"

"I do."

"Why?"

He said the first thing that occurred to him: "For example, you always used to love leafing through photo albums. Pictures of your father, your mother, your aunt somebody-or-other. Faded photographs of people who had died."

"What about you?"

"Me?"

"Yes. Weren't you always attached to your house and the people who had lived there? Now the house has gone, you're free. You don't remember, you probably never noticed, but in all our conversations… Well, it was rare for a day to go by without you talking about your house, your father, about Graça, Ginho, all of them. And when you weren't talking about them, Mateus, you would sit thinking, lost in thought."

"And is that why…" he began.

She flinched then in pain—real pain—and her whole face crumpled, and her hand shook, making the bracelets tinkle wildly.

"Why did you get out of bed? Isn't it time for your medicine, Alberta?"

Yes, she said, it was, adding that there was no reason for her not to get out of bed, given that she would be leaving in a few days. "I'll go and take my medicine now."

She went over to the door, but he asked again, "Is that why...?"

"No, not entirely," she said at once, like someone who has given the matter great thought. "That was the reason I gave myself, but no, that wasn't the real reason. I had always wanted to see the Acropolis."

She was incapable of lying right to the end. And yet all she needed to say was yes, and his pride as a man... But no. Alberta couldn't lie. That's why she had always been so defenseless against life. "I've lied to myself for days," she went on. "But it couldn't go on. I realized that. I'm just sorry to die like this, that's all. Here, after living a stupid life. I'm a complete egotist. All I think about is me and my body, about my death. And there's no reason to do that, is there? It will come anyway. But I just keep thinking, Mateus, thinking and thinking. Just remember, though, no drawers. If I come back that is. If I don't, there'll be no problem. And I'll have seen the Acropolis. You do understand, don't you?" She seemed anxious to hear his answer. She urgently needed that answer.

"Yes, I do."

She put her hand in her dressing-gown pocket and took out a ring, probably not a very valuable one. "I'd like you to have this before I set off. I don't care about the rest, they can keep that, but the ring…"

"Did your husband give it to you?"

"Yes. It belonged to his mother. I'd like…"

She was so clumsy, poor thing! How could she possibly have been happy in this world! He kissed her tenderly, with genuine tenderness, as if she were his sister, a slightly silly sister who had never learned to find her way around the city and was constantly getting lost in its labyrinthine streets. A very different sister than Natália.

"Of course, Alberta."

"Thank you." And she closed the door, and he heard her light footsteps moving off down the corridor. She still hadn't mentioned the phone call.

The following morning, Adérito Alves summoned him into his rather sumptuous office, furnished with a desk made from six feet of mahogany, a few ample green leather armchairs, and a carpet immune to footprints. Adérito seemed lost in thought.

"Now why the devil did I ask to see you?" he said at last. "And yet it was something urgent, important. Of course it was. But I have so many problems, that my memory... Ah, now I remember, at least this was one of many things, the most exigent." He stressed that last word, and Mateus thought that he must have read or heard it recently, and found it useful, suitably serious and with a certain pleasingly intellectual ring to it. "You and your colleagues are always thinking about other things, Silva. Your work's purely mechanical, and the less you think about it, the better. Am I right? Come on, tell me. What matters is football, or even politics, but football first and foremost—it's less divisive. Now I know you're one of the best workers here, but if I should fail to turn up one day, I really don't know what would ensue. Chaos." He paused to think. "My daughter's getting married, you know."

"So I heard, sir."

"Yes, and to a doctor. Apparently, he's a good doctor, but what use is a doctor to me? When I'm ill—because I'm not a well man, Silva, far from it—I go to my own doctor. So why would I need another doctor?"

"Of course, sir, you…"

"What a thing, eh?" He shook his head, as if he couldn't believe his own bad luck. "A doctor!" His booming voice filled the office.

Mateus expressed his deep regret. He did so without thinking, without even noticing, but he gave the impression, not seen, but felt, of someone profoundly sympathetic to Adérito Alves' woes. "It's my own fault, Silva," he blurted out. "It's my own fault, and no one can help me. My father was a peasant, and, to him, studying was synonymous with idleness. Work for him meant manual labor. He was a good man, but terribly limited. Fortunately, I had my mother, who really was an exceptional woman." He fell silent, as if in homage to her, and Mateus automatically stood up. An angel passed. It must have been the guardian angel of that woman or her son, the all-or-almost-all-powerful master of CIPPAR.

A thought came into Mateus's head: "My mother made hats, dozens, hundreds of hats," but he said nothing because his mother had no place there in the office of Adérito, a man so important that he could allow himself the luxury of having had a father who was a peasant and "terribly limited." "Having had," of course, not "having." Meanwhile, he—Mateus Silva to his boss—was in no position to boast of his mother having been a maker of hats. This is why he had always concealed the fact, and had never even told Alberta.

"Is there anything else, sir?"

"No, you can go, Silva, you can go."

Mateus went. When he sat down again at his desk, everyone eyed him curiously. Elsa asked, "Still in one piece? Not a single mark on you?"

"Still in one piece."

"But he felt ill, didn't he? He called for a doctor."

"No, no, the doctor is his future son-in-law. He's not a happy man, worried about his legacy."

"Ah, I see. The strong man who feels he's getting old, but who hasn't trained anyone to take over, because doing so could be dangerous, the pupil might supplant the teacher and then… But now, he thinks, is the time to give the matter some thought. He's wrong. The time has passed. His daughter is getting married, grandchildren will soon be on the way, his heart is beginning to fail. Who will be the heir apparent?" She giggled and said, "How they suffer, these poor, poor rich people! We should feel sorry for them, shouldn't we? I, for example, have nothing, absolutely nothing. What about you?"

I had a house, Mateus thought. A house like a sealed treasure chest of memories, Alberta said, to which there was no key. "No, I don't have anything either," he said, without looking at Elsa and thinking about a cheap ring (not the emerald ring, but the one with a simple Brazilian stone). "Absolutely nothing," he said.

Elsa observed him intently. She was a woman on her own, the same age as him, and she had worked there, across from him, for how many years? For seven hours a day, she was his most immediate landscape. The others said that she fancied him, that it was blindingly obvious. Perhaps it was. Mateus, though, pretended not to see or sense anything. He even rather liked her, but it went no further than that, he wasn't the kind of man to have affairs, and he saw Elsa only as a possible affair. Possible but not probable. One day, months ago, she had been rather tearful, and he'd consoled her as best as he could, from desk to desk. He could no longer recall what exactly he'd said, but he probably simply provided her with a good dose of platitudes, inherited or picked up from the ground like cigarette butts to be smoked by the destitute. She had many years ahead of her. Who knows, she might be very happy. Where there's life there's hope. Life is full of surprises. She was still young. Things like that.

She kept pressing the same key now, which she clearly enjoyed. "Yes, I'm really sorry for them. I feel for them. They're not free." (And are you free? thought Mateus. Free from what?)

"They live chained to their treasure or to the trunk of the money tree. They don't dare make a move in case someone comes and steals what belongs to them." (And do you dare to make a move? Where would you go? How? You don't have an Acropolis to visit. You're not tied to the money tree, but to the fig tree where one day you might hang yourself. Right there.)

"Do you know his daughter?"

"Only from what other people have told me."

"She was at the movies on that same night. She resembles a grasshopper in glasses."

"She's going to marry that doctor. And her father's really worried. What would he want a doctor for?" he said, his thoughts already far away.

Thinking about Natália. Perhaps she would turn up again one of these days. Because "she really needed to talk to him" again, but then, again, she would end up saying nothing. Or a lot? Without thinking, he smoothed his hair. He normally didn't give much importance to his hair or his tie, although he did to the crease in his trousers and the shine on his shoes. These details were essential to him feeling that he was decently dressed, that he was close to achieving ordinariness. As if being ordinary was his main objective. He was already neither handsome nor ugly, neither intelligent nor stupid, but he still needed to be neither elegant nor scruffy in order to place himself right in the middle, where we are less visible, less evident. The most distant point in someone's field of vision, seen from the perimeter, was therefore the optimal place for him. He noticed, though, that he had a small stain on his tie, which displeased him. Indeed, it displeased him so much that Elsa noticed, and immediately opened her left-hand drawer, in which she kept boxes small and large, bottles small and large, and liquids from Chanel No. 5 to alcohol to stain remover. She stood up, handkerchief in hand, proffering him that unpleasant smell.

"It'll come out in an instant, you'll see."

"You're an angel."

"I hope not. An angel, you say. Me, an angel? When I've committed so many imaginary crimes."

"You, Elsa?"

She sat down again, put away both handkerchief and stain remover, and sat sunk in thought while she pretended to put a new sheet of paper in her typewriter.

"Have I never told you about Hekk?"

"No, never."

"Well, Hekk, spelled H-e-k-k..."

"Yes?"

"Hekk is my small personal assassin. I always had one by my side, well, almost always. At first, he was a rather plump angel, but I soon realized that he wouldn't be much use to me as an angel, so I replaced him with a small elf the size of my hand, who later went on to become Superman. Recently, when things got really bad, I got myself a Venusian named Hekk, who was brilliant at sorting things out. He could make himself invisible and kill any awkward so-and-sos without a moment's hesitation. For him, killing wasn't a crime, but a perfectly natural act. On Venus, it was a perfectly natural thing to do, and he was brilliant at it. He would simply reach out his hand, and the person in question would crumble into dust. A tiny, colorless pinch of dust. No corpse, just one puff and they were gone."

"And you were completely innocent."

"Completely. With a more-than-clear conscience. That was Hekk. He would sit next to me or lie down at the foot of my bed. I found him in a sci-fi novel someone left behind in my house once, the only palpable memory they did leave behind. One day, I threw it out—the book that is—because whenever I looked at it, Hekk seemed less real."

"Did your Venusian kill many people?"

"The necessary number, the essential ones, I mean. He gave me many a peaceful night. Have you never tried spending several hours killing an awkward so-and-so?"

"Never."

"It's very satisfying and completely harmless."

"What happened to him?"

"To Hekk? I think he returned to base. Or died. Or just crumbled into nothing."

"Did he ever talk?"

"No, never. He was quiet as a mouse. But I could feel him nearby and that was great."

The typewriter began working again.

It happened the next day. It was suffocatingly hot—an oven with no sea breeze—and he, Mateus Silva, went so far as to unbutton his collar and loosen the knot in his tie. He was in a hurry to get home because Alberta was alone, but he had, without noticing, involuntarily, slowed down. Involuntarily? The streets were full of suntanned women wearing low-cut dresses, as there had been on the morning he'd gone to sell his house, and people seemed livelier and happier, as if they'd just burst into flower, as if they were preparing to bear fruit. At home, all that awaited him was gloom and the complaining voice of a woman he no longer loved—had he ever loved her?—whom he hadn't chosen from among other women, who had, as they say, merely happened. A woman he had found in a newspaper, then in the small living room of a third-floor apartment, and with whom he had stayed because her words and her gaze protected him, warmed him like a cocoon.

At the end of the street, almost on the corner, was a café, with tables and chairs spilling out onto the sidewalk. Mateus carried on straight ahead, but, at a certain point, he was obliged to step into the street because before him was a table, a chair, and a woman's tanned legs.

"Hello, Mateus!" It was her, of course. She wore a faint smile, the commas cutting deeper into her small face, her green hair falling onto her shoulders. Like a weeping willow, he thought. Or perhaps a pepper plant?

"Fancy seeing you here," he said for lack of anything better.

"As you see. I was waiting for you."

"Do you *really* need to talk to me?"

"Well, 'need' would be a bit of an exaggeration. And 'really'…no, not at all. I just wanted to see you, that would be nearer to the truth."

"Do you always tell the truth?" he asked.

"Sometimes. It depends."

She had stood up, leaving a few coins on the

table along with an empty bottle of beer and a glass.

"Shall we?"

"Why not?"

They walked for a while in silence. Then she said, "A few days ago—or weeks—I was at my parents' house, and a cat climbed up a tree. It was meowing for hours, and, in the end, the fire department had to come and get it down. It's easy climbing a tree, but coming down's another matter. I've been meowing for months and no one hears me. Apparently, all the firemen died."

He didn't know what to say, couldn't find the words. Natália was still walking beside him; he could see her profile slightly blurred by the light, her eyes lowered, still with that meaningless half-smile on her lips, and he thought about Alberta, who was preparing to climb down from her personal tree in order to die far away, having realized her childhood dream, a dream that the years hadn't faded, that had remained strong and intact. He thought of her and said, "You're not the only one, Natália."

She interrupted him. She was in the mood to talk, not listen. "Perhaps I just don't know how to meow properly, what do you think?"

"I don't think anything, but to be honest, it

doesn't seem to be that big a deal. We've met what… how many times? Three. And I wonder…"

He was wondering why she was wearing those strappy white sandals, with the straps crossing over her instep. He was wondering other things too. She, however, was talking. She launched into a confession, one that remained deliberately unclear so as not to be fully understood. A confession for personal use only. In short, a confession devoid of hard facts. There was a married man, his name didn't matter, Mateus wouldn't know him anyway. And what tormented her was that she had always dreamed of having a calm, organized life, yes, exactly, a bourgeois life, well, we're all different, and she—he must not forget—was the daughter of José and Graça Osório, the sister of Ginho—whom she called Jorge. She both wanted a bourgeois life and loathed it. She hated the idea of becoming like them, but…

"Basically, they're to blame. It was all so utterly phony. That's why I climbed over the wall and came to study in Lisbon."

"What did you come to study?"

"Oh, anything. The first thing that entered my head. He went to my first exhibition and bought a few pieces of ceramics. When I think about it now,

I guess he got me in that batch, too. You know the kind of thing, five for the price of four. The special offer that gets housewives all excited. I was the special offer. And here I am, a year later, living in the shadows, relegated to certain hours. We meet at my place because he's afraid his wife might find out. His wife has a bad heart. She won't live more than a year. And fool that I am, I believe him. I even believe his wife really does have a bad heart. I think that's why I came to see you."

"Because of that?"

"Because you're a sensible man, even if you did sell your house for half its value. Sensible, but not like them."

"Them?"

"Him. And my mother."

They were now walking slowly up the avenue. Mateus usually took the bus, but he didn't dare say anything, and allowed himself to be drawn along. He was listening to her. "If I understand you right, what you detest in them is the falseness of it all," he said at last.

"More or less."

"That's only normal. Just like your feet are the same as everyone else's feet. Mine for example."

She gave a deep sigh, as if she had finally managed to empty her lungs of the foul air filling them. "You noticed? I didn't think you would or maybe you'd have forgotten what I said. Do you think that…"

"I don't think anything. Why don't you talk to your mother?"

"She'd be shocked. Not ashamed, but shocked. Like when someone in the room tells a dirty joke. She'd be terribly shocked. My mother spends a lot of time with that ghastly Countess, she goes to mass on Sunday and is a bitter critic of young people nowadays and their free and easy ways."

"So, she doesn't know about your affair?"

"Even if she did, she would pretend not to, that's how she is. But I'm sure she really doesn't know about it. As for your father…I sometimes think…I really do…I sometimes think she's forgotten all about him, that she suffers from amnesia and has 'lost' certain things that happened in the past."

No, thought Mateus, she didn't lose them. She spoke to me about my father and told me what a great friend he had been. Unless she only remembers him as a friend.

"I sometimes think I hate other women. Perhaps

that's why I have no female friends. If you must know, I think they're horrible. I've always hated their radiant youth, their blossoming, their angry refusal to grow old, or… Nothing about them is natural, they're either all shy and withdrawn or else exhibitionists… I've never been able to talk to other women. I sometimes think that some women fall in love and get married and have children because that provides them with an inexhaustible source of things to talk about. I'm exaggerating, of course, but… About the suitors (some women, even at seventy, talk in public about the suitors they had, with no sense of the sheer absurdity of it), about the rich (or else handsome or famous) boyfriend, about giving birth (in lurid detail), their children's illnesses (every single one, always emphasizing their own extraordinary—remarkable—devotion), their children's grades, their successes, the teachers who loathed them or envied them, which is why they got bad grades. What are you thinking about?"

"Nothing, well, I…"

"I'm thirsty, do you mind if…"

"Not at all."

They sat down, and Natália ordered a beer.

"What about you?"

"All right, I'll join you."

He didn't like beer, but felt it was only polite to keep her company.

"My friends think I drink too much," she said. "But I drink thoughtfully. I think: I'm going to keep drinking until I reach that pleasant intermediate state of lucid mental freedom. Whole torrents of words come into my mind and I think and laugh like anything. It's all about myself of course—what I think and say—but, at the same time, it's free in the way a moored boat is free, only tethered by a long, long, long cable…"

She sipped some foam from her beer, which stayed on her lips. "Tell me about him."

"About who?"

"Who do you think? About your father. Who else have we been thinking about ever since we met?"

"But why, Natália?" he asked.

"I don't know! Does there have to be a reason for people to talk about a particular subject? Don't you know the playwright Ionesco?"

He didn't. Natália then began telling him about Ionesco, as if she had abruptly forgotten about the other man, a man named Abílio, who had loved a woman named Graça.

Mateus suddenly felt bereft of words and, still worse, of images. The void, with him spinning around inside it. Natália was talking about *The Bald Prima Donna*, but he understood nothing of what she was saying and didn't even try to understand. Then, gradually, the images began to surface again, strange, vague images. He remembered so little! His father in the Café Flor do Mar, with his gaze, at once absent and enthusiastic, fixed on Graça's beautiful face. His father scolding him because he had said "the Count's wife" instead of "the Countess." His father leaving the house at night. "I'm going to the café for a game of billiards, and I might drop by Osório's house. Do you want to come?" His mother shaking her head. "You know perfectly well that I don't like…" His father closing the front door. His footsteps out on the street, stopping outside the house next door. The muffled ring of a doorbell. A tall, fair-haired man. But was he really tall and fair-haired or was that just how he, as a small boy, had seen him? A broad, smooth forehead, hair gilded by the year-round sun, a wide, white smile. Was that what his father was like? Or was he an ordinary man, as ordinary as him, Mateus, ordinary and mediocre as that pillar in the square that he had once thought so unusual?

"Are you naturally blonde, Natália?"

"No."

"Ah."

His mother had never liked living in that town. She was from Lisbon, and, in her own eyes, this probably conferred on her a certain degree of importance. Apart from the Countess, to whom she had never spoken, and the local notables, who inevitably ignored her, everybody else, in her view, is a mere provincial. She had always been rather brusque. And, toward the end, this aspect of her became more pronounced. "Life," she would sometimes say. And that resigned acceptance, the humility it revealed, was painful to see. "Life." Life had been her husband, Graça, and later on, various furnished rooms and, finally, the fifth-floor apartment they'd had all to themselves, with the hats a constant presence, the hats that paid for their upkeep and for his studies. He recalled, as he often had before, the old top-floor apartment with sloping ceilings where, together, they had lived out the final years of her life. On the sparse far-more-than-secondhand furniture, on the beds, the chairs, the dining table, the floor, everywhere, there were lots of plain felt, soft muslin, yards and yards of fabric, colored feathers, mother-of-pearl or glass hatpins, light cobweb-thin veils. The ladies would be breathing hard when they rang the bell, and those sighs would lengthen or be repeated more gently as they came through the door. "Ah, dear lady, these stairs of yours will be the death of me. And, frankly, if I didn't like your work so much..." they would say. Almost all were over forty, which at the time he thought was ancient, and usually verging on plump. Pouter-pigeon breasts, short legs, delicate little feet, which a slight amount of swelling made even more sensitive. Maybe not all of them were like that, but some certainly were, the ones he remembered most clearly. His mother always had new styles to show them, which really pleased the ladies. "Oh, this one's lovely," they would say excitedly. "Now let's see what price you're going to ask me for it, because life is so difficult just now." "Very difficult," my mother would say. "But you'll see, it's not that expensive, and we won't fall out over it. And just look at the quality." He would sometimes arrive unexpectedly and stand there, staring at those absurd ladies wearing those incredible little hats. They, however, would have a satisfied, even smug expression on their faces as they studied themselves in the mirror flanked by two broken wall sconces. His mother would always say with great feeling, "Oh, it really suits you. It's not the kind of hat that would suit everyone, it must be said, but on you it looks wonderful. It's just your style." And it was clear that the ladies adored having "a style" of their own. Whenever he thought about his mother, he never imagined her on her deathbed. He imagined her bent over piles of straw or giving form to some piece of felt. She was always doing something, like Alberta when he first knew her.

"What are you thinking about? You haven't heard a word I've said, have you?" Natália said, drinking the last drop of her beer and quickly ordering another.

"I was thinking about my mother for some reason. You asked me to tell you about my father and then… She worked right up until the end. At the time, I was earning enough for both of us, but I don't think she would have known how to fill the time if she didn't have hats to make."

Natália was the first person he had ever told this to. She murmured, "There are women like that, it's a disease that afflicts only women. Sometimes I wonder, or perhaps fear…"

"What?"

"What job I'll end up doing."

"Didn't you tell me you were a ceramicist?"

"For the moment…"

"The moment?"

"Yes."

She fell silent, then said, "I'll probably take up something else when I get older. I'm not a very good ceramicist, far from it. I've had various exhibitions, but I only had any real success that first time. But so what? That's the way it is. I'm always terribly impressed, you know, when I see women carrying out household tasks with such dedication. It could be dusting, cooking the best chicken casserole in the world, methodically tidying drawers, making lace, taking lovers. They're perfect, aren't they? They put heart and soul into their work. Everything else becomes, in a way, secondary. Don't you think it's humiliating? Concentrating all that vital energy on such marginal, transient things. I mean, no one's going to die if there's dust on the furniture. Or if the supper's too salty. If the tablecloth isn't made of lace."

Or if they don't take a lover, he thought to himself.

Natália caught that thought. "No, that's another story. It's me, I'm always getting everything confused. Well, not always. Perhaps their job isn't taking a lover, but finding love. Then one day, when they realize it's all an illusion that will die a natural death—not love itself but the actual possibility of it lasting, even the urgent need for it—then those women devote themselves to being ladies. They sweep the past clean like someone sweeping the floor and continue on as if everyone had done the same. No looks, no memories can break the shell of their new but very robust dignity. It's unshakeable."

"So, you can't forgive her then?" he said.

She gave her usual throaty laugh, which always had very firm boundaries, at which it always stopped. "No, you're wrong. The only thing I can't forgive is the aura of cheap respectability she wraps around everything she says, her jibes about my life (of which she knows nothing) and what people might say because I live alone."

He hesitated, then asked, "How did you find out?"

"The usual stupid way, hard to believe really. We read cheap novels and think that... Letters, of course. Letters from Johannesburg. Why would she keep them, I wonder?"

"Perhaps to remind herself from time to time that she was once young and pretty."

"No, not even that. They were in the attic, mixed up with receipts and other bits of paperwork. She had simply forgotten them. She forgot the letters along with everything else." She paused, then asked, "Was she really so very pretty?"

"Very. She was, how can I put it…dazzling."

"Really? It's odd."

"What is?"

"Everything. Beauty, men, that word. She seems so right for her current role that I have difficulty imagining her in any other role. It's as if she's been playing this one for centuries, for whole eternities. Never a stumble, never a startled look in her eyes. Completely natural, as if these were old habits. And I know that's not true. I know there was your father. That there was someone else and then someone else. But by then, I had been born."

So, there had been someone else and then someone else. Mateus sighed. He was tired.

"You'd presumably like there to be some loud words of repentance, with much wailing and gnashing of teeth and spectacular acts of penance. Or at least the pale complexion and dark circles under the eyes of someone who spends many a sleepless night. It's her serenity you can't understand, isn't it?"

"Perhaps. Or perhaps I simply feel indignant at such a complete retirement from life, the kind of retirement awarded to certain good civil servants."

"Goodness, what a way to talk about your mother!"

"Why shouldn't I talk about her like that? I do love her, you know. She is perhaps the *only* person I love, apart from…well, apart from him, of course. But why should that prevent me from seeing her as she is? I was born under the sign of Virgo, and I have no illusions."

Mateus said gently, "No illusions, and yet you keep searching them out on the highways and byways."

"What if I do?"

"You might not find them."

"No, I might not."

She stood up, and so did he, having first summoned the waiter in order to pay. They walked side by side for a while, then she hailed a cab. She seemed to be suddenly in a hurry.

"Is it him?"

"Yes. And is your wife better?"

"No, just the same."

"We're all just the same, aren't we, and there's nothing we can do about it. I'm still up that tree, and who knows when I'll be able to climb down." She said this and got into the cab, slamming the door, without even asking if she could drop him off somewhere, without even having explained, in vague terms or all at once, what she wanted or hoped for from him. Some help maybe, but what? Just some help in continuing to exist? Maybe.

That night, Alberta said, "A few days ago, a woman called asking for you. Natália. Do you know a Natália? I forgot to tell you. She was, well, she seemed to be angry, is that right?"

"No, she was just up a tree meowing furiously, unable to get down."

"Like a cat?"

"More or less." He told Alberta about Natália. "She's convinced she's my sister. She needs to think that so she can..." He hesitated. "Perhaps just as a way of embellishing her story a little. Having an unknown brother would be romantic, wouldn't it? That would perhaps help her salvage her mother's image."

"And what about her father, that fellow Osório?"

"He's irrelevant. I suppose she also got herself

a married lover for the same reason, but that's just a supposition. She says she loves him, and maybe she does."

"I don't quite understand," said Alberta.

"Neither does she. Neither do I."

"I think I might have been a bit rude when she called. I was in pain."

"She thought you were jealous."

"Oh dear, you will explain it to her, won't you?"

"Of course."

"If she really is your sister..."

"I don't think she is, Alberta."

"Why not?"

"I don't know, but today I wanted to make sure... I don't know why, but... I'm not really interested in having her as a sister, to be honest."

"It would be good for you to have someone else when I..."

"Don't talk nonsense."

Alberta asked him to turn out the light. She was feeling very tired. What would she be thinking about? Would she make that trip? Would she? He doubted it. It seemed to him now that the train would be her bed. The ticket, on the other hand, that vague slip of paper she already had in her suitcase, and her passport would provide some consolation. Alberta was also up her own tree, one that she would never climb down from, no one would help her, not even him. One day she would fall, not like a cat, but like a bird with lead pellets in its belly. Or rather, since we're using metaphors, like a piece of rotten fruit.

Mateus locked himself in his room, a habit he would never lose. He rummaged around in drawers, took out some papers and put them back. He thought above all about how he would free himself from that other woman, now that life was about to free him—yes, yes, free him—from the woman in her room down the hall. He had always been honest with himself, so why shouldn't he be now? Whether Natália was or wasn't his sister had ceased to interest him. He thought for the first time that, despite selling his house, despite everything, he was basically a selfish man. What he wanted was a quiet life, his old habits, to live at ease with himself. Untroubled by his conscience. He didn't know what he should do, but he would find a way… He felt alone, free and melancholy. His gray, tepid, listless life would continue. And he would continue to live it, a grown-up for the first time. Ready to begin another life, whatever it might be, the same life.

MARIA JUDITE DE CARVALHO (1921–1998) published nine collections of short stories, a novella, and two collections of crónicas over her lifetime. She spent her career in journalism, working as an editor and columnist, and was also known for her French translations and paintings. Two Lines Press is the first publisher to make her books available in English.

MARGARET JULL COSTA has worked as a translator for over thirty years, translating the works of many Spanish and Portuguese writers, among them novelists (Javier Marías, José Saramago, Eça de Queiroz, and Teolinda Gersão) and poets (Fernando Pessoa, Sophia de Mello Breyner Andresen, Mário de Sá-Carneiro, and Ana Luísa Amaral). Her work has brought her many prizes, most recently the Premio Valle-Inclán for *On the Edge* by Rafael Chirbes.

www.ingramcontent.com/pod-product-compliance
Lightning Source LLC
Jackson TN
JSHW022138041125
93606JS00001B/1